Brinna stood fro...

The sounds stopped, as if the person who made them only just realized they'd been heard. The birds in the nearby trees were silent now, too.

"Who's out there?" she called after a moment. "You know you're not supposed to be here."

She half expected to hear footsteps scrambling away—some kid spooked to realize they'd been caught trespassing. Instead, there was only more silence. Brinna took a couple steps backward, inching closer to her car. She was probably overreacting, but she couldn't help the prickling sensation at the back of her neck.

Reaching for the door handle, she paused. Another sound caught her attention, and she whirled around to see the headlights of a car turning in at the front gate. Someone else had arrived. She was outnumbered now.

Worse, this other car was blocking her only way out.

Not the typical pastor's wife, **Susan Gee Heino** has been typing away since the first day her husband bought her a computer, hoping she would help with things like church bulletins. Instead, she found a passion for writing romance. A lifelong follower of Christ, Susan has two children in college and lives in rural Ohio. She spends her days herding cats and feeding chickens, crafting stories with hope, humor and happily-ever-afters. She invites you to visit her website at www.SusanGH.com and sign up for her newsletter.

Books by Susan Gee Heino

Love Inspired Suspense

A Dangerous Past

Love Inspired Cold Case

Grave Secrets
Texas Betrayal
Buried Threat

Visit the Author Profile page at LoveInspired.com.

A DANGEROUS PAST

SUSAN GEE HEINO

LOVE INSPIRED SUSPENSE
INSPIRATIONAL ROMANCE

LOVE INSPIRED® SUSPENSE
INSPIRATIONAL ROMANCE

ISBN-13: 978-1-335-63861-8

A Dangerous Past

Copyright © 2025 by Susan Gee Heino

Love Inspired
22 Adelaide St. West, 41st Floor
Toronto, Ontario M5H 4E3, Canada
www.LoveInspired.com

Printed in Lithuania

MIX
Paper | Supporting responsible forestry
FSC
www.fsc.org
FSC® C021394

He hath not dealt with us after our sins; nor
rewarded us according to our iniquities...
As far as the east is from the west, so far
hath he removed our transgressions from us.
—*Psalm* 103:10 & 12

Thank you to Audrey, Carolyn, Andrea, Jen
and all the wonderful librarians at the
Richwood-North Union Public Library
who are always eager to help me with research
and were happy to answer all my questions
about how things work behind the scenes.
Special thanks to Dustin Lowe for showing me
some of the amazing artifacts and documents
cataloged and preserved there to keep
our local history alive for generations to come.

ONE

Gabe Elliot checked the message on his phone again. He'd been called to the bedside of an elderly man named Mr. Kleinert. Gabe had only been in his position as part-time chaplain at New Minden Memorial Hospital for two weeks, but he was already finding the work more than rewarding.

Although he was new on the job, this hospital wasn't new to him. He'd grown up here in New Minden, gotten engaged to his high school sweetheart here, and then he'd run away.

He still wasn't sure if it had been more foolish to leave the way he did, or to think he could come back ten years later. But here he was.

His work at the hospital was a great way to embrace the community he'd once rejected. Straightening his collar, Gabe knocked softly at the doorframe. The door was open, so he stepped through. The elderly man in the bed turned watery eyes on him.

"Hello, Mr. Kleinert," Gabe introduced himself. "I'm Chaplain Gabe Elliot."

Mr. Kleinert nodded. His frail body was nearly engulfed in the hospital bed while machines hummed around him. There were tubes supplying oxygen and bags dripping saline and medications into his ailing body. Gabe pulled up a chair and leaned in, ready to offer whatever comfort he could.

He laid his hand gently over the old man's. "The nurses told me you asked for a visit today. Would you like me to pray with you? The Lord is always listening, especially in our times of need."

He was surprised when the old man summoned enough strength to shake his head and frown. His voice was weak but defiant. "No, the Lord stopped listening to me a long time ago. But people tell me you're a good man, so maybe He'll listen if *you* pray."

"How would you like me to pray for you, Mr. Kleinert? Are you struggling with pain?"

"Just the pain of my own guilty conscience," the man said, his words full of emotion. "I don't expect the Lord to forgive me, but maybe if I finally tell someone the truth, I'll have a little peace before I'm gone."

This wasn't the first time Gabe had comforted someone in their final days. It was only natural for people to be fearful when faced with the end.

Gabe's heart ached to hear the man's worry that he'd failed to measure up during his lifetime.

"The Lord's peace surpasses everything," Gabe assured him. "If there's something you want to talk about, He's listening, and so am I."

Mr. Kleinert's speech was slow, and his tired eyes drooped. "It's hard to remember. Sometimes it seems like it didn't happen, that it was all a hazy dream. Then it feels real again. It keeps coming back in foggy fragments, not a dream but a nightmare. I see it so clearly, though—it has to be true."

Gabe nodded, hoping his calm demeanor might soothe the agitated old man. He knew medications often interfered with a patient's grasp on reality, especially a patient as weak as Mr. Kleinert appeared to be. Perhaps the old man even suffered from mild dementia. Either way, Gabe was happy to do what he could to alleviate his fears.

"You've had a difficult time, and I understand that, Mr. Kleinert."

The old man chuckled, but that quickly turned into a coughing fit. He brushed away the glass of water Gabe offered him from the bedside table.

"Naw, you don't understand," he rasped. "I've got to tell you what I did all those years ago."

"It's all right. Whatever you did, God's waiting for each of us with open arms."

Gabe had never met Mr. Kleinert before, but

he'd gone to high school with two of the man's grandsons. That was twelve years ago now, but they'd been good guys. The whole Kleinert family was well-liked here in New Minden, active in church and trusted in business. It was hard to imagine this quiet old man had ever done anything to merit the unease and regret that was plaguing him today.

"Open arms, huh?" Mr. Kleinert said with a sigh, his head slowly relaxing back into his pillow. "I guess I'll be finding out soon enough. The doctors don't tell me much, but I see them whispering to my family. The cancer's nearly run its course, and I'll be checking out soon. This secret I've kept… I'll face the consequences for it. I just… I can't go to my maker without telling someone."

"That's why I'm here," Gabe assured him. "Burdens are lighter when we share them."

"But it's been fifty years! I went decades pushing it out of my mind. Now it's all I can think about. I hope if I tell you about it, they'll leave me alone."

"Who will leave you alone? Is someone bothering you?"

"The pictures in my head! The things I remember… I can't make them leave. I just want to forget, but I can't."

"These pictures in your head make you think you did something fifty years ago?"

"It's like a movie in my mind, playing over and over. I can't make it stop."

Like a movie… The poor man seemed to be struggling to recognize the difference between reality and some sort of fantasy, perhaps something he saw on television or in a theater. He might be suffering remorse for sins he hadn't even committed.

"Fifty years was a long time ago," Gabe said carefully. "If it doesn't seem real, maybe it wasn't?"

Mr. Kleinert shut his eyes tightly, and his lips trembled. When he spoke, his halting voice was full of emotion.

"It *was* real. It still is. Why won't you believe me?"

"I do believe you, sir. Please tell me what happened."

It hardly seemed fair to encourage the elderly man to continue, yet Gabe sensed that he needed to—whether or not his story was true. Mr. Kleinert's watery eyes peered directly at Gabe with sorrowful intensity. After a long, silent moment, he cleared his throat and spoke.

"I helped with it and got my hands dirty. It was as bad as it gets. It was murder." His words were soft, and Gabe struggled to hear.

"I'm sorry…did you say *murder*?"

"It was terrible," Mr. Kleinert confirmed. "Even in the dark, I could see it was too late. That man was a goner. I let him fade away while the angel of death watched from above."

Gabe tried to follow the old man's story. "Angel of death? I don't know, Mr. Kleinert. Maybe you should rest now."

"I can't rest! Didn't you hear what I said? I helped in a murder! I put him where no one will ever find him." His gaze darted around the room. "They murdered a man, and I helped them get away with it!" The fervor in his raspy voice caused him to break into another coughing fit.

Gabe wasn't sure what to do. He'd certainly not expected this. Whether or not Mr. Kleinert was delusional, the man clearly believed it had happened.

"I still see him lying there," the old man went on. "Blood is everywhere, and I feel sick from it. Blood on the floor, blood on the wall…and then blood in the dirt. I remember the dirt. I put him in that hole, and I covered him up. I'll never forget that. We thought if we didn't speak of it, the memories would all go away. They did for a while…but they're back. I just want to be rid of them."

"Who was there with you?" Gabe asked. "Who committed this murder?"

Mr. Kleinert's wild expression snapped into sanity. "Oh no, I won't tell you that. They'll face their maker in their own time, but I won't say any more. If you want to pray for me, you can. It won't change what happened, but I'm glad I finally told the truth."

"Wouldn't it help if you told me a bit more? In a matter like this, shouldn't the police—"

"No! No police. That's why I asked for the chaplain. You'll keep what I say in confidence. That's all I need, a listening ear and maybe a prayer. I've got to get these pictures out of my head...go to my end with a clean slate."

"Of course, we'll pray together, Mr. Kleinert, but this is something the police—"

"I said no!" The old man slapped his hand on the bed with surprising vigor. His voice was rising with every hoarse word he spoke. "I didn't call for the police then, and I won't do it now. This is between you, me, and God Almighty. Nobody else!"

Before Gabe could get more information from him, a nurse entered the room.

"Oh! I didn't realize you were in here, Chaplain," she said quickly. "I'll let you two finish up, but it's time for me to check your vitals, Mr. Kleinert."

"We're just about done here," Mr. Kleinert

said, his energy deflating. "The chaplain's going to pray for me. That's all he can do now."

The nurse nodded kindly. "That's very nice. And you have more visitors. I just ran into your granddaughter in the cafeteria. She's on her way up to see you with her friend. You remember Brinna Jenson?"

Mr. Kleinert didn't seem to recognize the name, but Gabe certainly did. His body tensed, and suddenly Mr. Kleinert's murder confession didn't seem like the biggest shock of the day.

Brinna Jenson was on her way up *here*? Now?

Gabe had never wanted to pray and dash so quickly in his life. But one look at the distraught old man, and he knew he had to get his mind back onto more important matters.

Mr. Kleinert was exhausted, defeated. His body sagged into the bedding, and his eyes glistened with anxious terror. He would likely pass from this life before long. How could Gabe simply dismiss the man's fear, despite the fantastic story?

Gabe's personal problems would have to take a back seat while he helped this hurting soul. Taking a deep breath, he reached for Mr. Kleinert's cold hand. "Let's come to the Lord now. He loves you so much and wants to bear your burdens."

This was what the old man needed to hear. He

smiled and sighed with relief. The nurse respect-fully left them alone, and Gabe began.

They prayed together, and Mr. Kleinert shed tears of repentance. Whether the story was the product of an aged and confused imagination or a medically induced fantasy, his remorse was sincere.

"Thank you," the old man said softly. "God bless you, Chaplain."

"I'll come back later to check on you," Gabe assured him before he left the room. "Rest well."

Mr. Kleinert was still smiling when Gabe headed out into the hallway. Even though this had been the most unusual bedside visitation, it felt good to have provided some comfort. His time with Mr. Kleinert had left him with two dilemmas, though.

The first dilemma was a matter of conscience. Mr. Kleinert had asked for a chaplain and expected to share his confession in confidence. However, it seemed he was unaware that hospital chaplain was only Gabe's part-time career. The rest of the time, Gabe worked for the local police. He was a cop.

When Gabe abandoned his life in New Minden ten years ago, he'd been a confused twenty-year-old kid. He'd taken off, joined the Army, and served his country. An incident that put him in a hospital bed had him asking himself difficult questions that eventually led him back to his faith. After his honorable discharge, he went through the police academy and served on a force in another state for several years.

Despite the fact that Gabe had promised never to follow in his father's footsteps and become a minister, the Lord called him, and he'd enrolled in seminary. He'd been ordained just six months ago. When his father faced some health issues and a spot opened up on the New Minden police force, Gabe knew the path was laid out for him. It was time to come home.

Now here he was, helping with his father's church, working part-time as hospital chaplain, and serving the community as an officer of the law. How could he simply ignore what he'd just heard? Murder was a heinous crime and needed to be investigated. Yet, how could he—in good conscience—put that frail, dying man through an interrogation? Would the Lord want him to do that? Gabe was honestly torn. He'd need to pray hard for some guidance.

His second dilemma, however, was much more pressing. It was a matter of sheer survival. The nurse had said Mr. Kleinert's granddaughter was on her way...with Brinna Jenson.

He wasn't sure he was up to it, but if the women were already on their way up, how could he avoid her? He'd better steer clear of the elevators. He'd take the stairs, instead. Mr. Kleinert had given him enough to worry about today.

He wasn't ready to face Brinna Jenson. Not yet.

New Minden wasn't a large town, and Gabe knew he would have to face her at some point. He'd been dreading it since he arrived back in town. What on earth could he say to the girl he'd once loved and had planned to marry? She had every reason to hate him for abandoning her the way he did.

Yes, he'd handled things very badly. He'd been young and stupid, though that was hardly an excuse. He'd loved her, but he hadn't been ready to settle down, and he'd been too much of a coward to tell her. If he had told her, she'd have let him go. She loved him that much, and he knew he wouldn't have been able to walk away if she set him free. It would've broken her heart, and seeing that would've broken him. He would've stayed…and made her miserable.

So, he'd taken the easy way out. He never had to see the pain in her eyes or the hurt that he caused. He'd simply left.

Two weeks before their wedding.

Brinna Jenson helped her best friend clear their lunch trays from the table. She'd been in the middle of a project at work, but Zoey had really wanted company today, so Brinna had agreed to take a break and meet up. Her job at the local library, overseeing the new wing that housed the Historical Society's local archives and the Minden County Museum, allowed Brinna the freedom to meet Zoey often for lunch. Zoey often said she was afraid if she didn't drag Brinna out of the archives occasionally, she'd get sucked into some dusty old history book and never be seen again.

But it was Brinna who was concerned about Zoey's well-being now. Today's lunch was in the hospital cafeteria. Zoey's grandfather was a patient here, and Brinna had come along for moral support. From what Zoey said, her grandfather wasn't doing so well. He probably didn't have long.

Brinna always remembered Dwight Kleinert as a kindly old man who'd cheered on the sidelines for Zoey and her cousins at all their sporting events when they were kids. It must be especially hard for the family to deal with his illness right now, just two weeks away from Zoey's big wedding.

"You still haven't got back to me about your plus-one for the reception," Zoey said.

"I know. I know," Brinna said. "But seriously, I'll be fine on my own. You're marrying my brother. It's not like I'll be lonely. I'm going to know everyone there."

"That's not the point," Zoey complained. "Isn't there someone—anyone—you want to bring? Won't you feel just a little bit awkward if you're the only one there alone?"

"I won't be alone. My whole family will be there. *Your* whole family will be there. Everyone we've known since early childhood will be there."

"Yeah…and maybe people we haven't seen for a while. Um, did your brother talk to you about the situation with the minister?"

Brinna paused before answering. She started to get a bad feeling about where this was heading. "No. What situation? Isn't Reverend Richards doing the ceremony?"

"He can't. His father-in-law is sick, so he's heading out to Iowa with his wife. No telling how long they'll be gone. He suggested we should ask someone else."

"There's got to be plenty of ministers available."

"You'd think, but it's June, Brinna. The wedding is two weeks away. Most everyone is booked up already. All except…"

"Except for *who*?"

"I know it might be weird for you, and the last thing I want to do is make you uncomfortable, but it's really last-minute, and he *is* a minister now, and since he just moved back to town, he's the only one open, and he *was* your brother's best friend…"

Brinna nearly dropped the tray she was carrying. Her chest tightened, yet somehow breathless words came spilling out. "You're going to ask *Gabe Elliot* to officiate your wedding!?"

Zoey cringed. "Um…if that's okay? Only if you're cool with it."

"You already asked him, didn't you?"

"Ben did. I'm sorry. We were getting desperate. But now you see why I think it's important for you to have a date for the wedding, right?"

"So I won't look like a sad little loser still pining for Gabe? No, Zoey, I don't need a date. I'm doing just fine without Gabe Elliot, and I don't need some random plus-one to make me feel special."

"You're okay that he'll be there?"

"It's not like I still sit around daydreaming about him. My life is great. I haven't thought about Gabe for years."

"Really? Even now that he's back in town?"

"I don't care if he's in New Minden or a thousand miles away. Gabe is ancient history for me."

"But you love ancient history."

"Not when it includes Gabe Elliot."

She was impressed with her confident tone. She sounded very secure. Even Zoey seemed to believe her, and she almost believed herself. Maybe it *was* true. Maybe she could be just fine standing there in the wedding party, seeing Gabe at the altar speaking the words and pronouncing Zoey and Ben man and wife. Maybe she wouldn't be swamped by the memories, melt down, and have a panic attack. Maybe she was finally over the guy.

She certainly hoped so.

They left the cafeteria and headed toward the elevators. Zoey pressed the Up button, and they stood waiting.

"I guess it's okay if you don't bring a date, but you're not allowed to bring a book and just sit there reading. I expect you to have a good time and... Oh no."

"Oh no, what?"

"I got salad dressing on my blouse. Wait here. I'll go get something to wipe it off."

Grumbling and fussing with her shirt, Zoey rushed back toward the cafeteria. Brinna sighed and stepped away from the elevators. Leaning against the wall next to the door marked Stairway, she pulled out her phone to make sure she wasn't needed back at work.

The summer reading program would kick off this weekend, so all sorts of preparations were underway for the annual open house. There would be games for children, educational displays, and Brinna would lead tours through the museum wing. When local businesswoman and philanthropist Carolyn Boyston passed away, she left funding and instructions for the wing to be added. It was the best thing that had ever happened to their little library.

Brinna had started working at the library when she was barely a teen. When she graduated high school, she was hired as full-time staff, and her life had felt perfect. She'd loved New Minden and never dreamed of leaving it. Why should she? She had a job she loved, a beautiful church, her family was here, and she was all set to marry her high school sweetheart. What more could there be to life than that?

A lot more, she'd found out.

Gabe left, and her little world crumbled. The future she had dreamed of and the life she had planned for simply ceased to exist. For a while, she'd been lost.

Thankfully, she'd not been alone. Her family and friends hadn't let her wallow in heartbreak forever. Eventually, she'd found the strength to make a new plan for her life. She still had her love of reading and studying history, so she'd bravely left New Minden and gone off to college.

It had opened her eyes. She'd discovered a whole world beyond their quaint little town. She'd met people who inspired her, saw things that amazed her, and welcomed a renewed thirst for learning. She outgrew her shy nature and did everything she could to forget all about Gabe Elliot.

She got her degree, traveled the world, and then came back to New Minden determined to help other young people learn and grow the way she had. Today, she had good friends, a satisfying job, a cute little house, and a three-legged tabby cat named Miss Mimi. She was happy, and no matter what Zoey said—or who officiated at that wedding—she was perfectly content. Gabe Elliot could walk right up to her now, and she'd feel nothing more for him than a twinge.

But she felt way more than a twinge when the door next to her flew open and slammed into her, knocking the phone from her hand. She staggered, clutching the wall and barely staying upright. What thoughtless clod would swing a door open into a busy lobby like that?

The clod apparently realized his mistake. He was already apologizing as he and Brinna both stooped to retrieve her dropped phone. His shoulder bashed into her head, sending her reeling again. She fell back against the wall as her knees buckled.

One look at his face, and she was glad the wall was there. She only hoped the solid concrete and cold marble of the building would be enough to hold her up.

"You!" She gasped.

"Oh. Hi, Brinna," he said.

That voice. It soaked right into her soul—through the tough outer shell she'd built, past the veneer of worldly education, slipping through her layers of confidence, and sliding deep down into the very core of her being. Her limbs froze, her heart pounded, and her lungs felt like they were filled with sand.

Gabe. She stood there staring at him, unable to move or to speak. Clearly, she had to take back all her brave words. She hadn't forgotten Gabe at all, and she was *not* ready to face him again.

"Um...sorry about that," he said. "Are you okay? It's good to see you."

"I just... I was... Can I have my phone back?"

"Here. I hope it's not broken."

He handed it to her, and she slid it into her pocket without even glancing at it. "It's fine."

Apparently, he was also fine. He didn't seem nearly as flustered as she felt. In fact, was he grinning at her? And what a grin it was...

It was the same smile that used to make her knees go weak. But she detected an edge to it now—something harder, more mature, more confident. His eyes were still just as blue, but there was an intensity in them that didn't used to be there. His jawline was different, too. More set, more solid. And was that a slight scar?

Indeed, Gabe Elliot was much changed from

the boy she had known years ago. Then again, she hadn't exactly stayed the same, either. She reminded herself she was very different from the girl he'd left. She hoped he could recognize that. She also hoped he hadn't seen the shock she felt at finding him here, the swirl of emotions that threatened to drown her.

She cleared her throat, but her voice still came out far croakier than anticipated.

"I'd heard you were back in New Minden."

"For two weeks now," he said, graciously ignoring her croak. "My dad needed help at the church, and there was an opening in the police department, so here I am."

He didn't seem to be struggling at all to form sensible words. He wasn't relying on the wall to keep him on his feet, either. How could he seem so calm and collected while the whole world tilted on its axis? Did he feel any of the things that she felt right now? She couldn't tell. All she knew was she had to get hold of herself. Gabe was here now, and she had to handle it. Somehow.

"Um... Zoey says you'll be officiating at their wedding," she blurted.

"Yeah," he replied. "I'm really happy to be a part of it. I always knew those two would get together."

She was *not* ready to discuss Ben and Zoey's love story with him. She didn't even want to think of romance, weddings, or happily-ever-afters while he was standing here.

"What brings you to the hospital?" she asked.

"I'm part-time chaplain here." He touched the clerical collar he was wearing.

"Oh. Of course," she said, embarrassed by her silly question and yet thrilled to have a reason to get out of this conversation. "You're working. I'll let you go. I have to get back to work, too."

"At the library, right?" he asked. "You're in charge of that new history wing, aren't you?"

She tried not to look pleased he knew about that. "Yes, the Carolyn Boyston History Center and Minden County Museum."

"That's great. It's right up your alley. In fact... would you be able to help me search for some information?"

"What sort of information?"

"I'm interested in finding information about something that happened locally a while back."

While she may not be happy to prolong this uncomfortable meeting, she did love talking about her job. "We have lots of local information. What time period are you interested in?"

"Roughly fifty years ago."

"That should be easy enough. We've got old newspapers, genealogy records, agricultural reports. What kind of documents will you need?"

"I don't really know," he said, shaking his

head. "I'm looking for evidence of a possible crime. Where do you think I should start? Was there anything big going on around here fifty years ago?"

She paused, meeting his gaze to make sure she understood what he was asking.

"You mean, anything other than the huge scandal at the Boyston factory?" she asked. "The one where a million dollars went missing, and my grandfather allegedly bankrupted half of the town?"

He blinked at her. Clearly, her words had caught him off guard. "*That* happened fifty years ago?"

He knew what she was talking about. Everyone in New Minden had heard the stories. There were still places where her family wasn't welcome because of what her grandfather had done back then. Or rather, what he'd been accused of doing. He always claimed he was innocent, but no one outside the family had ever believed him. Some New Minden folks never recovered from the financial disaster that followed her grandfather's catastrophic failure as a manager at the old Boyston cabinet factory. Brinna's own mother still refused to talk about it.

"Yeah, that's when it went down," she said, her words clipped. "You want to study up on my grandfather? That scandal is the crime you're investigating?"

"No… I'm sure this has nothing to do with him. Probably. Maybe."

"What sort of crime are you researching that happened fifty years ago and probably maybe doesn't have anything to do with my grandfather?"

Now it was his turn to clear his throat and show signs of discomfort.

"Murder," he replied.

TWO

"Murder?" Brinna couldn't quite grasp the word. "You're saying you think my grandfather could be involved in a *murder*?"

"No, of course not."

"Then who was?"

"I don't even know if there *was* a murder," he said, making no sense at all. "That's what I'm trying to find out."

She huffed in frustration. "Aren't you a cop? Shouldn't you already have that information?"

"It wasn't reported. *That's* why I need to do research."

"If it wasn't reported, how are you going to research it?"

He sighed and shifted his weight from one foot to the other. "That's where I'm hoping you can come in, Brinna. I need your help."

He still wasn't making any sense, but she wasn't entirely sure if that was his fault or hers. Was Gabe Elliot actually asking her to help him?

He'd turned her life upside down ten years ago, and now he was just going to waltz back into town and ask for her help? If that was indeed what he was doing, she was really looking forward to telling him no.

Before she had opportunity, though, he went on.

"You're in charge of the county archives, right? I don't know where else to start investigating something like this. You must have records or historical documents we can look at that might let us know if somebody from town went missing back then."

Her head was practically spinning. He needed her help professionally. It was her job to do exactly what he was asking for. She tried not to let the frustration show on her face.

"Yes, we probably have resources to help with your search."

"Great. When would be a good time to meet up there?"

"Meet up? Um…you don't really need me for this. I'll get one of the reference librarians to help you out."

He frowned at her words. "I'd rather not bring anyone else onto the project. At least, not until I know for sure if—"

His words cut off, and Brinna followed his gaze to notice Zoey making a beeline toward them. She was beaming.

"Well, look at you two. What a surprise. Catching up, are you?"

"We bumped into each other," Brinna said, hoping the glare she shot her friend would be enough to stop her from saying anything embarrassing.

Zoey ignored the warning. "It's almost like old times. How are you, Gabe? And how's your dad? We've all been praying for him after he had his stroke last month."

Brinna realized she should have said something about his father's stroke. Reverend Elliot was an important part of New Minden's community, and they were all very worried about him. It was no secret the reverend's health challenges were the reason Gabe had moved back here. Gabe was living with him, helping at the church, and making sure his father got the care he needed. From what she'd heard, it was a blessing he had survived at all.

"He's doing pretty well, thanks," Gabe replied. "He's been home from the hospital for a week now and is getting back most of his speech and motor skills. We've still got a way to go before he's back to normal, but God has been gracious. Now we can focus on happier events, like somebody's upcoming wedding."

Zoey glowed as he brought up this topic. "Can

you believe it's finally going to happen? We really appreciate that you'll be officiating for us."

"I'm honored to be a part of it. Knowing you, this will be the wedding of the century for New Minden. Ben says you're inviting half the town."

Zoey laughed, and Gabe seemed so completely at ease. He chatted and joked as if they were all the best of friends, as if everyone had simply forgotten the way he left. How could he be so comfortable? Brinna was still trying to calm her nerves.

Zoey seemed as unbothered as Gabe. "Not quite half the town, but nearly. We both have big families, and we both work for Boyston Industries. I'm in quality control over at the factory, while Ben's up in the ivory tower there. You know, corporate headquarters with the bigwigs."

"Ben always did have grand plans," Gabe replied. "He'll probably be running that place someday."

"That's his intention," Zoey said. "He's made himself indispensable to the current CEO. I don't know how they'll get along without him while we're on our honeymoon."

The two of them laughed. Brinna glanced around to see if any passersby had noticed their little group. Mostly, she wondered if anyone casually watching them would recognize how uncomfortable she felt. Zoey and Gabe might be enjoying this reunion, but Brinna was not. She took a deep breath and inserted herself into the conversation while she had the chance.

"They'll find a way," Brinna said sharply. "The Boystons always do. But come on, we've got to visit your grandfather now. I'm sure he's eager to see you."

"Oh, he can wait a few more minutes," Zoey said. "It looked like you and Gabe were in deep conversation, and I wouldn't want to interrupt."

"No, just small talk. We can go now," Brinna insisted.

Zoey raised an interested eyebrow. "Small talk about what?"

"Work," Gabe replied. "I need to research some local history, and I've heard her new wing of the library is packed with that kind of information."

Zoey practically tripped over herself to brag about Brinna's work. "Brinna is the queen of local history. Representatives come from other libraries and historical societies all over the state to see what she's done here. If you need to research something, she's your girl. Of course you'll help him, won't you, Brinna?"

Brinna just rolled her eyes as Zoey and Gabe both turned to her expectantly. "I'm pretty busy right now…"

"I'm happy to work around your schedule,"

Gabe said. "What time will you be back at the library? I'll stop by, and we can look at your calendar."

"That sounds perfect," Zoey chimed before Brinna could think up an excuse. "I'll have her back there in an hour. Less if my grandfather is too tired to visit long."

"Wonderful," Gabe said, thanking Zoey although his gaze never quite left Brinna. "It's a date."

Her mouth popped open to assure him it was *not* a date, but Zoey grabbed her arm and pulled her toward the elevator. There was nothing Brinna could do but purse her lips and give Gabe a glare that assured him she wasn't happy with the arrangements he had just made. She honestly couldn't tell if the awkward smile he gave her was the result of nerves or if he was actually looking forward to meeting up with her later.

Well, she wasn't looking forward to it. She'd do her job, though. If Gabe really was researching a murder from fifty years ago, she would help him find the information he needed. She was an adult and a professional, so she would behave like one. She didn't have to like it, though.

If Gabe thought she could just forget what he did ten years ago and carry on as if they were nothing more than old friends, he was terribly mistaken. Her faith had helped her learn to forgive him, but she wouldn't let herself get close to him again. Or trust him. But she would help him with his investigation.

Not a lot of big things happened in New Minden, and if there had been a murder at the same time as the scandal involving her grandfather, it was just too huge a coincidence.

Brinna would help Gabe, but she would help herself, too. She'd find out what he was investigating and make sure he didn't dredge up old pain, old rumors, and old hatred. She would not let her grandfather be vilified all over again.

THREE

Brinna was glad Zoey's grandfather wasn't up for much small talk. He didn't want much conversation at all, in fact, and kept apologizing for all the trouble he was putting his family through. Zoey assured him over and over that he had nothing to apologize for, but he shook his head sadly. He seemed very tired, so they didn't stay long.

Brinna stepped into the hall to take a call from work, and Zoey joined her after just a few minutes. She was clearly upset, and Brinna knew it was hard for her to see the old man this way.

Poor Mr. Kleinert. All her life, Brinna had known him as a pillar of his family. It was painful to see him so diminished now, so disconnected from everything. Brinna knew Zoey was broken up over it, but Zoey wasn't ready to talk about it. It was impossible not to wonder if Mr. Kleinert would still be around for the wedding.

Zoey hardly said two words as she drove Brinna back to the library. It was just as well. With Zoey too upset to talk about her grandfather, she also hadn't insisted on talking about Gabe.

Brinna really didn't want to talk about him. She didn't want to think about him, either, but it seemed her brain had other ideas. Even her efforts to dive back into work didn't help. Not when the recently donated collection of wartime correspondence she was sorting turned out to contain tender love notes sent from Private Bosey Dutton to his sweetheart back home, Patricia Hallis.

While it was more than endearing to read through them and watch the relationship blossom while young Bosey was off fighting in Europe and Pat waited anxiously here, their flowery words of devotion brought back bittersweet memories for Brinna. Her own sweetheart had put on a uniform and gone off to fight, but she'd had no letters from him. There had been no notes to comfort her, no words of affection or promise, and no hope for a joyous reunion. Every page Brinna archived reminded her how much she had hurt ten years ago.

The lovers were reunited at last when the war came to an end. They married and raised a family here in New Minden, celebrating peace and fifty-seven happy years together before Bosey passed away. Pat followed him three years later, and the letters had remained cherished by the family ever since. Now the grandchildren were sharing them with the community.

It was a lovely gesture and a wonderful addition to the museum. Brinna only wished she were in a better frame of mind to go through them all. She boxed up the letters carefully and set them aside. She needed something to distract her...

Her gaze fell on the microfilm reader. Maybe a quick scan through some old newspaper articles would get her mind off her past heartbreak. Gabe said the supposed murder he wanted to investigate happened fifty years ago. There would certainly be news articles from that time. It might be a good idea to peruse them and see if she could find anything related to his concerns.

It was easy to find articles regarding the scandal at Boyston Industries fifty years ago. The local paper had followed it closely. The company had been preparing for a major expansion that would mean more jobs and prosperity for the town, but then evidence of fraud and embezzlement came to light. Brinna's grandfather was blamed for it—either by his direct actions or gross negligence and incompetence—and the whole project had come to a halt.

Boyston had nearly gone bankrupt, and over half of the employees had lost their jobs. Brinna had grown up knowing this story, but she'd never actually dug in and researched it for herself. Perhaps Gabe's so-called murder investigation wasn't such a bad thing after all. It had inspired Brinna to look into the matter, and she might find the information to finally exonerate her grandfather.

She was deeply engrossed in her research when someone interrupted her.

"I see you started without me."

It was Gabe. She'd been so focused on her work that she hadn't heard him enter the room. Her insides made an involuntary flutter when she glanced up from the film reader to find him smiling at her. She frowned at him and checked the clock on the wall.

"I figured you'd be here sooner, if this was really such an important investigation," she said.

Her intentional rudeness slid right by him, and his smile didn't fade. "I guess we're both busy people. So, what have you found so far?"

"Nothing, of course. I have no idea what I'm looking for."

"A possible murder from fifty years ago."

"Right. But it wasn't reported to police, and therefore probably wasn't in the newspaper. How do you even know there was a murder?"

"I don't. That's why we are investigating."

"But why are we investigating in the first place? How did you find out about it?"

He was quiet for a while before he answered. "I can't really divulge much, but…someone confessed to me."

"Someone?"

"I can't tell you who. That's confidential."

"A murder confession is confidential? Is there some kind of new law or something?"

"Look, they didn't confess to me as a cop, but as a minister, okay? And they didn't confess to committing a murder, only to knowing about it and helping cover it up."

"Fifty years ago."

"Right."

"So it would have to be someone well over fifty years old."

"I can't tell you who it was. I can just say I'm not entirely sure they're in their right mind. They might have dreamed this whole thing up. I can't very well put this person and their family through an interrogation if it's just a delusion, so I need to quietly do some research to find out if there was a murder back then. You understand?"

"I guess so. But how do we find a murder that might not even have happened?"

"We'll look for missing persons, unclaimed property, people with violent histories. I can access some of that in the police database, but if it wasn't an official case, it won't be there."

"So you need to scour old news articles. Okay, I've got some microfilm loaded from that era. Ready to dig in?"

He glanced at the notepad she'd been scribbling on. She always took notes when she researched a topic, but she doubted he would make heads or tails out of her penmanship.

"I was just compiling a time line for major events in the year you mentioned," she explained. "So far, there's nothing that says murder."

Despite her sloppy handwriting, he seemed intrigued by her notes. He pulled up a chair next to her, picked up her notebook, and scanned it carefully. Her first impulse was to grab it back from him, but that would be childish. She had agreed to help him on this, so there was no reason not to share her notes, even if it felt awkward to share anything with Gabe Elliot.

"I see your grandfather had just been promoted to plant manager at the new facility they were building."

"You can read my chicken scratch?" she said, mildly surprised. "Yes, he was. It was a great opportunity for him. At least, it would've been. A guy from the wrong side of the tracks working his way up from nothing and becoming plant manager. Too bad he didn't come from one of the more important families in New Minden. When the scandal broke, and the Boystons needed a scapegoat, it was easy to pin it all on him."

"You think that's what happened?"

"Of course that's what happened. My grandfather is a good man. He's honest, hardworking, reliable. There's no way he would have stolen from the company or sat back and let anyone else do it. They made him out to be a thief—a crafty con artist who lined his pockets instead of doing his job. When no evidence could be found to prove that, they shifted the story to say he was lazy and incompetent, that he looked the other way while someone else stole the money. None of that is true."

"I believe you. Your grandfather is a great guy. So who did they decide stole the money while he looked the other way?"

She shrugged. "No one. I never heard they tried to pin it on anyone besides my grandfather. I've been reading through the articles printed about it, but it seems like the story just went away."

"How does a story like that just go away?"

"Good question. I'm up to newspapers printed six months after the scandal, and the headlines are all about the economy and national news, not much about Boyston Industries."

"Want another set of eyes to help you read?"

"Sure, but I warn you, it's easy to get distracted and lose focus. You should see some of the ridiculous advertisements they had back then. And the articles on the social pages are so much fun, describing what the teenagers wore to the homecoming dance, announcements about Mr. and Mrs. Schroeder taking their new station wagon all the way into the big city for the day, letters to the editor complaining about the shocking addition of a second traffic light in town… It's a gold mine. I keep forgetting what I'm supposed to be looking for."

He laughed with her and pulled up a chair at the microfilm reader next to hers.

"Maybe it's not such a good idea to have a history buff doing the research," he said. "I'll try to use my cop brain and stay on task here."

"Oh, sure, I dare you to ignore the full-page ads from the local car dealer with all the hottest new models back then. I know how you love classic cars. Even your cop brain won't be able to resist those."

"Then I guess we'll both enjoy the work," he said.

She set up his machine and gave him a quick tutorial on how it worked. He seemed to know what he was doing, so she forced herself to relax. This was his investigation, after all. She should be thankful he was the kind of man who would take the time to search for the truth. Someone else might have dropped the matter as soon as it was evident there were no police records.

The fact that he seemed to honestly believe her about her grandfather's innocence was a big positive, too. As awkward as it was to sit beside him after all this time, she was glad for his presence.

His mysterious investigation might be a blessing in disguise if it helped her grandfather.

She took a deep breath to calm her nerves and turned back to studying her own machine. There were two newspapers in New Minden fifty years ago, so she'd given a set of microfilm from one newspaper to Gabe while she would continue with the other. If there was any hint of a murder back then, they were sure to find it.

They went through article after article, occasionally reading paragraphs to each other when something of potential interest popped up. Brinna took notes, but other than tracking names and dates of any people involved in the scandal at Boyston Industries, she didn't have much to write down. Most of what she found told her what she already knew.

As she predicted, Gabe did enjoy the car ads from fifty years ago. They laughed together as he read car descriptions along with prices that seemed absurdly low compared to modern costs. They laughed at the society pages too, as names of people thcy knew popped up in wedding and engagement announcements. Occasionally, they'd peer into each other's film reader to see old photos of mutual acquaintances in their younger days.

All in all, Brinna was surprised by how easy it was to work with Gabe. It was almost like spending a day with an old friend rather than the man who so cruelly broke her heart. How had he wormed his way back into her good graces so easily? Helping him professionally was one thing, but she had no intention of becoming friends with him again. Maybe they'd done enough research for one day.

"Look, I think I need a break from this," she said, pushing back from her machine and standing.

"Yeah, I'm starting to go cross-eyed," he replied. "Do you think we found anything useful?"

She glanced at her notebook and shrugged. "It doesn't feel like it. I've got a list of names of people who were interviewed regarding the trouble at Boyston, and there were a few reports of other crimes in the area, but I can't say any of that really points to a possible murder. What do you think?"

"I think I should've been taking notes, too," he replied. "This article here does a good job of listing the financial discrepancies at the time and the Boyston personnel who had access to banking. Is there any way I could get a copy of it?"

"Yes, we can print from these machines. Just line it up on the article you want, and we can send it to the printer in the back room."

She leaned over to show him how to do all of that. He seemed intrigued by the process and even suggested a couple other articles he was interested in. He was taking this investigation seriously.

"Okay, if that's all you need, the printer is back here."

She led him from the main archives room through an Employees Only door and into the workroom. It was a wonderful space with room for plenty of storage and a wide table for her various projects. The printer was at the back wall beside a binding machine and a light table. A locked cabinet held her sealing supplies, small tools, and various solutions for cleaning and restoring old documents. When Mrs. Boyston bequeathed this new wing for the library, she'd made sure to provide funds for all the bells and whistles.

"This looks like cutting-edge stuff," Gabe commented, glancing around the room. "What does that machine do?"

"Believe it or not, it's called an ultrasonic welding machine," she replied.

She loved watching people's confused reactions when she said that, and Gabe did not let her down.

"*Welding?* What on earth are you welding in a library?"

"It's for encapsulating documents, fragile papers that need to be preserved." She pointed out the various items used in the process as she gave a quick explanation. "Say you've got some very important paper item from a hundred years ago—a contract or a newspaper clipping, or even something not flat, like a book. You need to protect it, right? So, we put it between sheets of archival polyester and then seal that around it. Presto. Your item is preserved."

"This heats the edges of the polyester and fuses it?"

"It fuses it, but not with heat—you can't use heat on a precious old artifact. Instead, it uses energy pulses."

"You mean, like sound waves?"

"Yes, low-frequency sound waves. It's the safest way. It's pretty high-tech and expensive, but good old Mrs. Boyston wasn't one to cut corners. When she was setting up her legacy to create this historical center, her advisors told her we should have one of these, so she put it in her bequest."

"Do you actually use it?"

"Of course. The original signed charter for New Minden is hanging over the front desk, carefully encapsulated. We've got several old family Bibles that were donated to us that are encapsulated for preservation. Once you've got the equipment, the process is fairly simple and inexpensive. Also, it can be easily undone if you need to examine the article. We do a lot of work for other libraries, museums, and archives, too.

Not everyone had piles of Boyston money to set them up, so we help out where we can."

"That's pretty nice," he said. "Who knew cataloging a bunch of old stuff could be so complicated."

She cringed at his words. He probably didn't mean anything by them, but she'd heard that sentiment before. People who didn't understand what she did tended to think of her as nothing more than a glorified file clerk, someone who alphabetized things all day and shushed noisy children in the nonfiction section. Hearing Gabe disregard her life's work carried an extra sting, and she took a deep breath to regain her composure.

"Here's the printer."

Gabe's copies sat in a neat pile, so she collected them for him. He was clueless to the insult he'd dealt her, so she tried to let it roll off her back. She wasn't in this to impress people, after all. She did her work because it was important and because she loved it.

"Did everything come out okay?" she asked as she handed him the copies.

"Yeah, they're fine. It's a pretty nice setup you've got. Is that your office over there?"

"Did the name on the door tip you off?" she asked, not quite able to avoid a hint of sarcasm.

"Whoa, look at all those credentials hanging

on your wall. Very impressive, Brinna. Good for you."

Once again, he sounded surprised she'd made something of herself. Why did she let that hurt her so much? What should have been more painful, in fact, was the realization that none of those credentials would be hanging there today if he hadn't left her the way he did.

Somehow, she'd gotten over her loss and discovered a love of learning. The life she'd made without Gabe was a good one. She liked who she'd become, and it hardly mattered what path she'd taken to get here. Instead of resenting Gabe for what he'd done, she realized for the first time that a part of her was actually grateful.

Not that she had any intention of telling him, though.

"So are those articles all you need?" she asked quickly.

"Yeah, thanks. Wow, you've got a lot of things in here. Is all this stuff that's been donated for the historical center?"

She realized it must look like piles of random junk, but all the artifacts she had here were carefully sorted and waiting for restoration and cataloging. Some would be put on display and some would be put into storage, but all would be recorded. He seemed to be interested, so she took a moment to reply.

"Yes, families and organizations donate things they believe are important to the community. This box over here, for example, came in last week. My brother brought it in. They're all items from Boyston Industries. He found it while they were cleaning out storage areas in their old office facility."

Gabe glanced through the box and pulled out an item. It was made of thick, circular glass with a wooden frame. The whole thing sat on turned legs about four inches tall. He held it up to look through it, the curved glass making his eye appear unnaturally huge.

"This is kind of fun," he said. "What is it?"

She laughed. "An old desk magnifier. It rested on the desk, and you moved it around over whatever you wanted to study. Much more convenient than holding a glass in your hand."

"Ah. What about this?" He pulled out another object. This one was shiny metal made to look like molded gold. It was about eight inches tall and sat on a small marble base with a plaque on it.

"That's one of the awards Carolyn Boyston received, the Singularity Award for exceptional service and philanthropy. I think she got one every year. This one is broken, though. See how it's shaped sort of like a horse's head?"

"It's abstract, but I can see that."

"Well, it's supposed to be a unicorn. I guess the horn was broken off. That's probably why it's in the box rather than displayed on a shelf somewhere."

"Can you fix it?"

"I'm not sure yet, but I'll see what I can do. It doesn't matter much, though. Carolyn had dozens of these. She always kept the newest one on her desk, but the others had their own cabinet."

"Well, this one's fifty years old. Does that make it more valuable?"

"I don't know. Do you want to get back to the investigation?"

"Okay, I'll quit playing with your artifacts."

"You're such a grown-up," she said, hoping he couldn't tell she was actually amused.

She led him out of the workroom and back into the main area. A shadow in the doorway caught her attention. At least, she thought it did, but when she went to peer out into the hallway, no one was there. Obviously, spending so much time with Gabe was messing with her mind.

She joined him back at the film readers to re-file everything properly. He was studying his machine with a frown.

"What's the matter?" she asked.

"It's just that… Well, I was looking at a film from July earlier, but now the film showing up is a newspaper from October."

"These things are pretty sensitive," she explained. "There are a lot of newspapers on one film. You must've bumped the viewer when we left, scrolling it from July up to October."

"That seems like an awfully hard bump," he said, frowning. "Check your machine. Does it look right?"

She didn't see the point of it, but she humored him and leaned in to view the film still loaded in her machine. As expected, it was right where she left it.

"Mine's fine. You obviously bumped yours. It happens."

"Yeah, I guess so. Well, could I get a quick photo of your notes there? Maybe I can take them back to the station and run some of those names through the database to see what pops up."

"Good idea," she said, moving her notebook forward so he could snap a clear picture of it with his phone.

"Thanks," he said. "And thanks for the eye-opening tutorial on what goes on behind the scenes here. You've got a pretty cool job, Brinna. I can see why you're so good at it. Can I stop by again tomorrow to look through more of these old newspapers?"

So he *did* have a measure of appreciation for what she did. He might've just redeemed himself the tiniest bit from his earlier slight.

"I'm pretty busy getting some new donations logged in and sorted, but you can stop by, and I'll help if I can."

"Great. Thanks a lot. If there was someone murdered here fifty years ago, I have no doubt we'll find some kind of clue in your archives."

She nodded, and they said their goodbyes, but she called for him just before he walked out the door.

"Just so you know, I'm mostly doing this for my grandfather. I need to know you're not going to let all the rumors and hearsay sway you into implicating my grandfather. Promise me you won't get caught up following any so-called clues that might damage his name."

She met his gaze but couldn't read it. He took a long pause—too long—before answering.

"I can't do that, Brinna," he said softly. "I can't make that promise."

Her heart sank, and an icy cold washed over her. Of course he wouldn't promise her. She'd been foolish to ask. The last person she should have turned to for a promise was Gabe Elliot.

She watched in silence as he simply turned and walked away.

FOUR

Gabe tried to keep his mind off Brinna when he returned to his office at the police department, but that was impossible. She really had done very well for herself, and it was obvious she'd found her true calling. He couldn't deny he was a bit jealous. Despite the fact that he'd made his own career and come back to his faith, he still felt something was missing. Brinna, however, seemed content.

He was proud of his service to his country, the work he did now as a police officer. Of course, he was so very blessed to be in the ministry, too. Sharing the Lord with others and being available to them for counsel and support was the highest calling he could ever have. Having lost his mother at an early age, he struggled with his faith and made huge mistakes. The fact that God had saved him and walked with him through the dark times to bring him back here today was a gift he would never take for granted.

But Brinna seemed to have something he did not. Whatever it was, he admired her for it. She didn't need to help him with his research, but she'd done it. Despite their past, she'd been kind to him. At least, kinder than she had to be.

Gabe had noticed a chill in her voice more than once, but she hadn't been rude or dismissive. She'd been friendly for the most part. If only he hadn't left things on a sour note with her.

But she knew he was a cop. She couldn't ask him to compromise his investigation. Maybe it would turn out to be a moot point. As he searched the names from her notes in the police database, he didn't find anything that led to her grandfather—or to anyone, really. The people mentioned in the newspaper articles seemed to all be Boyston employees who knew nothing about the missing money.

Since no one else could be implicated, the blame all fell on Brinna's grandfather. Without evidence, though, he was never charged. Not that the general public had cared about due process. As far as his coworkers and neighbors were concerned, many were out of a job because of him.

Gabe typed in name after name. He looked up the various members of the Boyston family who ran the place at the time: Clement Boyston, head of the family and CEO of the company; Carolyn Boyston, his wife and the real rock who kept the company going; and Shirley Boyston-Jones, their daughter who was fresh out of college at the time of the scandal. As expected, Dwight Kleinert's name showed up, too.

They'd all given statements at one time or another, although nothing they'd said had offered any indication a murder may have occurred. No mention was made of any missing person at all. The only thing missing seemed to be money, and that had never turned up. In a small town like New Minden, people would've noticed if someone had come into a million dollars.

So what really happened back then?

Gabe clearly wasn't any closer to figuring it out. He rubbed his temples, shutting his aching eyes and rolling his shoulders to release the tension that had been building. After hours at the computer, he needed a break.

Glancing out the window, he realized the sun had sunk below the trees lining his street. It was nearly seven thirty already, long after his shift officially ended. Family friend, Kay Hefler, had gone over to have dinner with Gabe's dad tonight. She was a godsend. Recently retired from nursing, Kay had been coming around a lot and looking out for Dad since he'd had the stroke. Gabe honestly didn't know what they'd do without her.

But it was time for him to head home for the

day. Any clues about what had happened fifty long years ago would still be here to find in the morning—if they existed at all. Gabe stifled a yawn and watched the light evening traffic on the quiet street.

Something caught his eye... Or rather, some-one. Just to the right, he could see the corner of the library building. Brinna came into view. She crossed the street and headed to her car parked in the municipal lot directly across from the police station. She still looked as fresh and put-together as she had when he'd seen her earlier in the day. Her curly dark hair was still tied up neatly in her usual ponytail, and it bounced as she made her way toward her car.

Something else caught Gabe's eye. A man—someone Gabe didn't recognize was also watching Brinna. The man was several rows over in the parking lot, leaning against a car. His features were indistinct at this distance and he wore a ballcap, but his head turned as Brinna passed, confirming that he was staring.

But what was suspicious about that? Brinna was an attractive woman. It was rude of the man to stare, but how could Gabe blame him when he'd been standing here doing exactly the same thing? Still, he had a funny feeling about the guy. Maybe it was pure jealousy, but maybe it was something more.

That feeling was confirmed when the man hopped into his own car at the very same time Brinna got into hers. His running lights came on at the same time hers did, too, and as she began pulling out of her parking space, he did the same. When he turned his car the same direction as hers, Gabe knew he wasn't imagining things.

The man was following Brinna, and she had no idea.

Gabe grabbed his car keys and took off. It was a quick dash to his personal car parked in the police lot. But would he be quick enough to track Brinna? He didn't even know where she lived.

He refused to think of all the scenarios that might unfold. Surely he was overreacting. New Minden was a safe place. Brinna was leaving a public parking lot on a peaceful evening, not prowling a dark alley in the middle of the night. But why were Gabe's senses all suddenly on high alert?

He didn't need to know why. He just needed to act. Pulling his personal vehicle out of the police parking lot, he scanned the street. At first, he panicked, then he calmed down when he recognized Brinna's car. She'd driven onto Green Street and was waiting at the traffic light with her turn signal on. The man in the other car was right behind her. Gabe waited, and sure enough, when the light changed and Brinna turned left, the man followed.

Gabe did, too.

He kept his speed low, letting the other two cars remain a casual distance ahead of him. At the last stoplight in town, she turned right on the state route. The man was still right behind her. Gabe closed some of the gap between them. They were leaving the populated area, and there weren't many buildings out here. As the sun sank lower and the shadows grew, he couldn't help but worry. Why was she headed out of town all alone with a stranger on her heels?

As the drivers slowed to navigate a curve, Gabe got just close enough to the man's car to catch the plate number. He recognized a sticker in the car's window, too. This was a rental car. That was interesting. There was only one rental agency here in town, so it wouldn't be hard to track this guy down if it turned out Gabe needed to. For now, though, the man wasn't doing anything wrong. Gabe intended to keep it that way.

He followed the two of them as they continued down the road. The landscape on both sides was nothing but farmland and scattered residential homes now. Gabe was surprised when Brinna's car began flashing a turn signal. She was slowing down and obviously preparing to turn into the driveway of one of the homes. Did she live all the way out here? Gabe waited, watching the other car intently. Would the man turn into the driveway with Brinna?

He didn't.

Gabe breathed a sigh of relief as Brinna pulled into the driveway of an older farmhouse, while the man in the other car continued straight ahead. Gabe's fears were unfounded. It must have been a coincidence that the man had watched Brinna walk through the parking lot, then driven out after her.

There were other cars in the driveway where Brinna stopped, and Gabe watched in his rear-view mirror as someone waved at her from the front porch. It seemed this wasn't Brinna's house, but she must have stopped by to visit someone. Good. She wouldn't be alone. Just in case the other car really had been intentionally following her, Gabe was glad to know she was in a safe place.

He leaned back and let the car ahead of him get some distance between them. Now that there was no more cause for alarm, he felt a bit foolish. Why had he jumped to the conclusion the man was following Brinna? There was no real reason to be suspicious. Maybe it had been pure jealousy right from the start.

Well, that didn't say much for Gabe's plans to put the past behind him and start a fresh new life, did it? One thing this little jaunt had proven was that he clearly hadn't gotten over Brinna. Taking a deep breath and letting it out slowly, he tried to release his concerns.

The horizon was bright with a wash of color as the sun continued to set. Gabe turned onto the next road, thinking maybe a little quiet time would settle his nerves and put his mind back on the right track.

He turned on some music, rolled down his windows, and let the warm air rush over him as he drove through the countryside. He recognized landmarks, houses of old friends, and he marveled at the many new homes that had sprung up over the past ten years. So much of New Minden was exactly the same, but so much had changed.

Brinna had changed, too. He couldn't quite get his mind off her. To be honest, he didn't really want to. He liked thinking about her, remembering the good times. If only those thoughts didn't eventually lead to remembering how he'd messed everything up.

Somehow, though, God had brought him through. Gabe couldn't take credit for the path his life was on today. God's grace had certainly caught him off guard. To be honest, he was still a little bit surprised to be here, back in New Minden, working with his father in the church. Their relationship hadn't been especially close over the past years, and Gabe's return hadn't magically made things better. But he was where he was supposed to be. He knew that with certainty.

Gabe needed to put his past failures behind him once and for all, and that included coming to terms with his regrets. He'd tried to convince himself he didn't really regret walking away from Brinna, that it had been the right thing to do. Now he knew he'd been lying to himself.

He'd been wrong to walk away then, and he'd be lying if he said he was over her. He wasn't. If he had any hope for truly moving forward and making a new life, he needed to deal with that.

He wasn't sure what his future in New Minden would look like without Brinna at the center of it, but one look at her happy, successful life today proved that's how it would be. She'd moved on and built a great life without him. Now he needed to do the same.

Brinna smiled at Mr. and Mrs. Gelhaus as they waved goodbye from their front porch. She'd stopped in to drop off some books for them after work. Mrs. Gelhaus didn't drive, and Mr. Gelhaus had been in a tractor accident last month, so he still wasn't getting around very well. They were such faithful patrons, so Brinna and some of the other library staff took turns making deliveries and picking up returns for them. It was just one of the many wonderful perks of being in a small town.

As she pulled out onto the county road, she carefully checked for oncoming traffic. There was no one in sight, unlike the parade of cars that had followed her on the drive out here.

That had been odd, and she really had felt she was being followed. With the glare from the setting sun on the car windshields, she hadn't been able to see who was inside. When she'd pulled in at the Gelhauses, though, the cars had driven peacefully by. She'd chided herself for considering someone might have been tailing her.

Why had her mind jumped to that conclusion? Maybe because she'd noticed one of the cars had pulled out of the lot next to the police station. A small part of her had hoped it might be Gabe. She sighed at her own foolishness.

Why would she want Gabe to follow her? She didn't want that, of course. It was bad enough that she'd agreed to help him with this so-called investigation. Did he really believe a murder had been committed? Well, so far there was no evidence to back that up. All they'd done was search through a lot of painful reminders of a really difficult time for Brinna's family.

She'd grown up hearing snippets about it from her family. It was a part of her life, but she'd really had no idea how bad it had been. After reading through those articles in the newspaper, she understood it better.

She knew her grandfather was innocent, but she couldn't prove anything. It seemed the same for Gabe's murder investigation. He couldn't prove a murder had even occurred. Would he be content with that conclusion? Was there something else she could do to find more information?

Taking the long way back toward town, Brinna sighed in frustration. She should be glad Gabe's investigation was hitting a dead end so soon. He'd be out of her hair, and this whole topic would just go away without dragging her grandfather's good name through the mud. Again.

Even now, well after eight o'clock at night, the June sunset was bright. Brinna was thoroughly enjoying these longer days as summer geared up. The landscape around her was a contrast of deep shadows and rays of golden light. Fields of winter wheat waved vibrant green, and freshly turned soil showed rows of bean and corn seedlings. New life was all around her.

She turned onto Tuft Farm Road that would take her back into town. The road would take her past one huge reminder of just how real the scandal fifty years ago had been. The new Boyston factory her grandfather was set to manage was supposed to have been built out here, a mile outside of town, with the hopes that the facility would need space to grow. There had been great expectations for the new facility, and for Brinna's grandfather. No one could've known it would end so badly.

Well, she corrected herself, *someone must have known*. Someone had been embezzling that money, putting the company's future at risk. But who?

Binna rounded a curve and could see the tree line ahead that signaled the old factory's location. A dilapidated fence ran around the perimeter of the property, but it was in such disrepair that it kept nothing in or out. What was once an impressive building site with expansive parking areas was now just a bare lot with a few beams suggesting the outline of the industrial structure that would have been.

Today, the site was all overgrown. Shrubs and trees grew through the broken pavement, and litter collected in the weeds, discarded by trespassers and blown into piles by the wind. Local young people came out here. Brinna herself had visited countless times. It was the perfect place to avoid teachers and parents for a while.

She smiled at the recollections. Her group of friends had never really gotten up to mischief. They'd just poked around and found the occasional broken tool from construction years ago. She'd come out here with Gabe a few times alone.

They had gazed at the stars and talked about their future together. It had felt like they had it all figured out back then. It was easy to feel blessed, to assume God only ever answered Brinna's prayers with a hearty *yes*.

Then everything changed. Her world had shattered when Gabe left. It felt like the floor dropped away beneath her feet and she would never stop falling. Not only had God stopped answering her prayers, but she wasn't even sure he still heard them. For a time, she stopped praying.

Was that how her grandfather had felt when the floor dropped out beneath him? How had it been for Brinna's grandmother, for her own mother, who had been a child at the time? Their lives must have felt ruined, their faith in God shaken.

Somehow, they'd endured. Brinna's grandfather was the strongest person she knew. He lived a life of faith and devotion to God, and that was shared by his wife and his daughter. Brinna had never considered that they all must have wrestled with their faith during those difficult years. When she'd gone through her own dark times, they'd been there to help her through. Their prayers and their love had guided her back to faith and showed her that even though Gabe might have left, God never did.

Without even thinking about it, Brinna slowed her car and pulled into the gravel patch that had once been the entrance to the facility. The gate had been pushed open and left hanging sideways. Already a mulberry sapling had grown up through it. How odd that this ruined site had played such a pivotal part in her family's life for three generations now.

Ever since Gabe left, she'd avoided the place. She avoided the memories, too. Tonight, though, it was time to face them. For whatever reason, Gabe was back in her life. What better place to start unpacking that baggage than here, where past and present trauma collided?

She got out of her car and soaked in the cool, dewy air. Birds rustled in the trees around her, settling for the night. In front of her loomed what was left of Grandpa's factory, its walls mostly gone, and its metal girders silhouetted like a dark skeleton against the sky.

A bat fluttered past, and Brinna ducked, then chuckled. It was as if this place was trying to be as forlorn and foreboding as possible. No wonder it was irresistible to the local teens.

The building itself had been months away from completion when the scandal broke, and everything had come to a halt. Exterior walls had been put up, but not the interior ones. Only the office area had been walled in, creating a place for her grandfather and the foreman to work, with a large area where the payroll department would be. A

sturdy safe had been installed there, or so everyone said. Brinna had never asked her grandfather to confirm that—maybe because she didn't
want to know, and maybe because she knew her
grandfather hated talking about anything to do
with that time.

Legends and lore abounded about this place.
Kids loved to whisper about it, to suggest all
sorts of alternate histories for the site. One story
Brinna heard often was that since the missing
money had never been found, maybe it was still
here, still in that safe. Periodically groups of teens
would prowl around, searching for the elusive
safe and its hoard of stolen cash. A legend had
sprung up, claiming some otherworldly specter
was protecting it, and it could only be found on
the night of the full moon, or something like that.

Brinna had never believed any of those tales.
Surely if the safe existed, and if the money was
ever in it, the investigators would've found it
fifty years ago. People just liked to have things
to imagine.

Wait…what was that noise? Was Brinna imagining *that*? She didn't think so. Something was
moving in the underbrush around the factory
ruins, something large.

It sounded like footsteps. She heard leaves
crumbling, twigs snapping… Brinna was almost
certain someone was coming toward her in the

darkness. But who would be here? She didn't see any other cars. Could someone have come to the site on the old access road at the back of the property? What were they doing here?

She didn't hear the usual laughter or hushed joking of teens, but she certainly had heard something. She stood frozen, listening carefully. The sounds stopped, as if the person who'd made them had realized they'd been heard. The birds in the nearby trees were silent now, too.

"Who's out there?" she called after a moment. "You're not supposed to be here."

She half expected to hear some spooked kid caught trespassing scramble away. Instead, there was only more silence. Brinna took a couple steps backward, inching closer to her car. She was probably overreacting, but she couldn't help the prickling sensation at the back of her neck.

Reaching for the door handle, she paused. Another sound caught her attention, and she whirled around to see headlights of a car turning in at the front gate. Someone else had arrived. She was outnumbered now.

Worse, this other car was blocking her only way out.

FIVE

Brinna's heart pounded. Had she accidentally stumbled into some illicit meetup? If it was just kids, why hadn't the first person identified themselves? Who was this newest arrival, and just how nervous should she be?

As the car crunched closer over the gravel, there were still no additional sounds from the person she'd heard in the darkness. She opened her car door, and the interior lights came on, spilling around her. The approaching car was very near now and stopped. The driver's door opened and a man stepped out.

"Brinna?"

It was Gabe. She had never been so happy to see him.

"What are you doing here?" she asked.

He sounded as surprised to see her as she was to see him. Due to the growing darkness and broken shadows from the ruined building behind them, she wasn't certain she could read his expression, but she thought she detected a smile there.

"I was just driving around and thought I'd pull in and see what was left of the place. You?"

"Um…pretty much the same. You weren't coming out here to meet someone?"

"No, who would I meet out here? Oh, wait… are you out here to meet someone? Have I interrupted?"

"No! Of course not. I just…" She dropped her voice low and moved closer to him. "I think someone's here. I heard footsteps."

His head jerked up, his gaze scanning the area. "Where?"

She waved her arm in the general direction the sounds had come from. "Out there somewhere. I couldn't quite tell. It was just…someone was walking around, rustling leaves and branches."

There were no sounds now, just the hushed breeze and the crunch of Gabe's own feet on gravel as he moved toward the shadows, listening and watching.

"You didn't see them?" he asked finally.

"No, but it's probably just kids…or something."

"Did you see or hear a car drive in after you?"

"No."

"Okay, then. I'm sure they weren't following you."

"Following me? Who would do that?"

She felt an involuntary shudder of fear at his words. Why would he even think such a thing? No one would follow her. Then again, why had she thought the same thing just a bit earlier on her drive out?

"I don't know. I don't see a car, so they must've already been here, right?"

"Or maybe I imagined it all. There certainly doesn't seem to be anyone else around here now."

As if to prove her wrong, they heard the sudden rumble of a car engine start up just beyond the ruined shell of the factory. Flashes of headlights shone through the underbrush. Someone else had been here. The shadows shifted and writhed with the motion of the headlights as the car turned around. The red glow of taillights faded and disappeared.

"I guess whoever it was, they're leaving by that old access road," Gabe stated.

"Maybe we spooked them," she said. "Kids. Now they'll have some new story to tell their friends of a scary visit out here."

"Yeah, they'll turn us into headless horsemen or something. You okay?"

"I am, thanks. I shouldn't have even come out here. Sneaking around isn't nearly the thrill that it was a dozen years ago."

He chuckled at her words, no doubt thinking back to his own memories of that time. "True. We really thought we were getting away with something then, didn't we? Driving out here, meeting up with friends, playing our music too loud and talking like we owned the world."

Her laughter was a little more bittersweet than his. "We sure thought we had it all figured out back then. What did we really know of the world, though?"

"Sometimes I feel like I know less about it now than I did then, and I've been on four continents."

"Wow, you soldiers really get around. Where did they send you?"

He shrugged, as if his service was old news and not worth talking about. Or maybe he didn't like talking about it. She'd heard he'd been injured at one point, but he was obviously fine now. Then again, how could she know that? There was no telling what he'd been through. Maybe she shouldn't have asked about it at all.

"I was in Germany for a while, did some training in Japan, and there was Afghanistan."

"Is that where you were injured?" she asked, hesitant to pursue the conversation, but curious.

"You heard about that?"

"Only through the grapevine. I know your dad went to stay with you in Maryland while you recovered for a while. But… I guess you're okay now?"

"Yeah. I can't go through airport security without setting off some alarms, but I got to keep my leg."

"That sounds pretty serious."

He merely shrugged. She knew him well enough to recognize this topic was off-limits. Whatever he'd been through, this pain wasn't something he was ready to revisit. Not with her, at least.

"I'm very blessed," he said simply. "I know guys who… Well, let's say I don't take my life for granted anymore. How about you? I heard you've done some world traveling, too."

"I have. I did a summer study program at the British Museum after my first year of college and got hooked on travel after that. Now I work with high school students and take a group on a tour of historical sites every summer."

"Every summer? Where will your group be going this year?"

"Oh, this year is special. We're going to New York to study the life of none other than Aldridge Boyston."

"Boyston? Any relation to Boyston Industries?"

"Aldridge Boyston started the company here way back in 1905. He came to America in 1890 at the ripe old age of fifteen and became a cabinetmaker's apprentice in New York. We're going to trace his journey through Ellis Island and learn about the immigrants who came over here in the nineteenth century. A lot of the kids in our group are going to look up the names of some of their ancestors in the database there."

"That sounds very educational."

"There will be fun stuff, too," she assured him. "We'll see a Broadway show, go to the top of Rockefeller Plaza, and have a picnic in Central Park."

"It's New York City. You won't have any trouble finding things to do, that's for sure."

"The trouble is narrowing it down to what we can see in just one week. Do you know how many amazing museums are right there in Manhattan? That's not even counting the fascinating sites in the other four boroughs. Deciding what to see and what to skip is always the hardest part of planning these trips."

"It's a pretty big world, that's for sure."

"It is. So you've been to four continents? Obviously, you're including North America, and you were in Germany, so that covers Europe. Afghanistan and Japan are in Asia, so that's three. What's the fourth continent?"

"Africa," he replied. "After I recovered and finished my time in the Army, I went to seminary. Through a friend there, I learned about a mission group building schools and medical centers in Ghana. It just felt like something I was supposed to do, so I went and had the honor of working with some wonderful people last year. It helped me get my head together again."

"That's great, Gabe. I'm sure you helped a lot of people there."

"I hope to go back again sometime. But hey, don't you think it's about time we head back to civilization now? Your stalker seems to be gone now."

"If anything, they probably thought *I* was the stalker," she said, hoping she sounded light-hearted despite her lingering nervousness on the subject. "Whatever they were up to, I'm the one who interrupted them."

"Well, I'm just glad they left without giving you any trouble."

"I owe you some thanks for that. Until you got here, all I heard was footsteps getting closer in the darkness. Then you pulled up, and they must have tiptoed back to their car pretty quickly."

"Whatever they were up to, they didn't want to deal with the two of us."

"And I wasn't eager to deal with them. Yeah, it's time to head home. It was silly to come out here anyway."

"First you thank me, now you call me silly? I came out here too, you know."

She was glad to hear the teasing tone in his voice. "I know, I know. We both ended up out here for whatever reason, but now it's time to head back."

"Well, then, I guess I'd better move my car out of your way. It's good to visit the old place again, though. I'm glad it's still standing."

She glanced up at the hulking frame looming over them. The sun was fully set now, and stars dotted the dark sky. It was almost like old times, the two of them out here, the constellations glittering overhead… Yet it was also nothing like old times. She and Gabe used to be so close, like one mind with one goal. Now the space between them was nearly as huge as the sky above.

"What's left of it is still standing," she corrected.

He sighed. "At least there's that. Maybe someday they'll do something with it."

"No, it's been too long. What happened here destroyed any hope for a future. There's nothing left worth saving."

He paused before his reply. "Yeah, you're probably right. Okay then, let's head out. It was good to see you again, Brinna. You still up for meeting tomorrow to dig into more records?"

"Sure. We need to know what really happened."

"We do," he agreed.

He gave her one of his irresistible smiles before sliding back into his car. She dropped into hers, pulled the door shut, and took a deep breath. She wasn't sure what should have rattled her more— hearing an unknown stranger creeping toward her in the dark, or wishing Gabe had disagreed when she declared there was nothing here worth saving.

Gabe backed out of the gravel lane and allowed Brinna to pull out in front of him. It would have been pointless to try to catch that other car, given where the old access road would have come out. Best to just make sure Brinna got back to town safely.

The roads were dark all around them and he stayed behind her as they came to the first traffic light in town, then he followed her past the library and the police station to the next intersection. He had to make a decision there when she signaled she was turning left. Would he follow even though that wasn't directly on his route home?

She might think he was overstepping, that he was prying into her life if he followed her. Then again, she had seemed nervous about the mysterious person she'd encountered at the old factory site. Maybe she would be glad for the escort, as long as he didn't make a big deal out of it.

He'd just follow her to her driveway, then wave and be on his way when it was clear she was safely at home. Yes, that was what he'd do, and not just because he was nosy about where she lived now.

This had been an unusual day, to say the least. Murder confessions, bittersweet reunions, and strangers prowling in the dark certainly made it easy to be a bit jumpy.

He turned his car to follow hers. She drove a couple blocks and then started heading up Mulberry Street. Gabe chuckled to himself. Brinna always dreamed of a cozy house on Mulberry Street. She'd done it, hadn't she? She'd made her own dream come true.

Mature trees lined the street, and two-story homes from a bygone era looked down on them from either side. They were built by middle-class professionals during New Minden's early days and had been updated and restored by subsequent generations. In the daylight, passersby would be treated to green lawns and gardens springing up with early flowers.

Tonight, it was dark. Huge trees cast broad shadows over everything. Brinna's car slowed in front of one of the houses, and he realized she was pulling into a driveway. This must be her home. Gabe studied it as she turned, and her headlights swung over it to illuminate the welcoming front porch and the white picket fence.

In a flash, the headlights shone on something

else—a dark figure lurked near the front steps. A person was clearly there, although Gabe only caught a glimpse of him. Yes, he was sure it was a man. Was he wearing a ballcap? And had he been peering into Brinna's front window?

Brinna's car was in the driveway now, blocking Gabe's view. When he could see the house again, the figure was gone. Gabe pulled his car up to the curb and grabbed the flashlight he kept on hand. He leaped out of the car, cleared the picket fence, and shone his light across the front of her house and the large porch. No sign of anyone.

Brinna had also gotten out of her car. She came rushing toward Gabe while he rummaged through the azalea shrubs under the window where he had seen the man. He was just about to order Brinna back to her car when she called to him.

"You saw him, too!"

"Yeah, I saw a guy, but just for a second."

"I thought I must have imagined it," she said, breathless as she flicked on the light from her phone and joined Gabe in his search. "It looked like he was right around here."

"I don't see him now, though," Gabe said with a sigh. "No sign of tampering at the window, although there are a couple partial footprints. If he was trying to get in, he didn't succeed. No telling where he went. Any idea who it was?"

"No, I didn't get a good enough look at him," she replied. "I couldn't see his face, but maybe he's one of my neighbors."

"Snooping around your front yard, looking in your windows?"

She shrugged and wrapped her arms around herself in the cool air. "I couldn't really tell what he was doing. Maybe just someone looking for a lost cat in the bushes. It's not exactly a high crime rate area here."

"No, but after someone was following you around the old factory site—"

"Someone was there, but they couldn't have been following me," she interrupted. "They had to have already been there when I arrived, or I would've heard their car drive up. That was just a coincidence."

He hated the word *coincidence*. Especially when it was getting hard to believe this could be one.

"A coincidence like the guy who waited in the parking lot and then followed you out of town earlier tonight, huh?" he asked.

Her eyes went very large. "So that was *you* coming out of the police station. Yeah, I recognize your car now. You *were* following me."

"No, I was following the man who was following you. Didn't you notice that other car?"

"I noticed a car, yes, but so what? It was the

end of the day. Lots of people were going home from work. It's a small town, and it's not unthinkable that a couple of us would drive in the same direction at the same time."

"Yet you noticed my car coming from the police station and following, too. Obviously, three cars in a row seemed odd enough that you didn't instantly forget about it."

"All right, I did wonder about it," she said with a sigh. "I did sort of feel like I was being followed, but then I got to the Gelhaus's, and the other cars kept going, so I assumed I was just being paranoid. But—"

She stopped when a noise from inside the house caught their attention. There was a loud thump, and it sounded like something crashed to the floor. Gabe's adrenaline surged. It was clear from Brinna's expression that she was as startled as he was.

"Is there supposed to be anyone in there?" he asked.

She shook her head, looking nervous and perplexed. Maybe he'd been too quick to think that the man they'd seen at the front of the house had run away. Or maybe he wasn't alone. What if their prowler had a partner inside, ransacking Brinna's house? Worse, what if Gabe hadn't seen the shadow out front and just driven on by, leaving Brinna here on her own?

"Stay here," he said quietly. "I'm going in."

"It's my house. I'm going in, too," she declared.

The determination on her face assured him it would be pointless to argue. He was caught off guard again by this new self-assured version of Brinna. She was aware of the danger just as much as he was, yet she didn't shrink back. He admired that, but he worried. What were they dealing with? He couldn't afford to let her walk into danger.

"At least let me go first, okay?" he said.

"First, you'll need me to unlock the door," she amended.

"Fine, unlock it, but stay back."

He fought off a cold chill at the thought of what—or who—could be waiting inside, hoping to catch Brinna alone.

SIX

Brinna led Gabe to the door at the side of the house. He was glad she didn't simply charge ahead, but paused to let him get a good look at things. Neither of them spoke as he inspected the door, checking it for tampering or signs of a break-in. It seemed in order, so he motioned for her to try her key. It slid into the lock easily, and the doorknob turned with no trouble. He held up a hand to motion for her to allow him to step in ahead of her. She rolled her eyes but let him pass.

He was glad he'd just come from work and was still in his uniform and fully armed. Stepping over the dark threshold, he fumbled at the wall for a light switch.

"It's over here," she whispered, scooting in beside him.

He caught the scent of her hair—fresh with a hint of something flowery, lavender maybe. His whole being reacted to the sudden close proximity to her. Waves of memories washed over him, and he took a step away. Her nearness and warmth were too much.

She'd reached her arm past him and flicked on the switch. Light poured over them, and he blinked as his eyes adjusted. They were in a tidy kitchen. Lace curtains hung at the window, and a potted violet sat on the small round table. A simple overhead fixture in the center of the room glowed, illuminating the kitchen and contrasting with the darkness in the rooms beyond. He took a deep breath and regained his composure.

"The sound came from that way," he said, staying as quiet as possible. "What's through there?"

"The living room," she replied, her voice calm and soft.

He took a step toward the arched doorway that opened into the next room. She followed behind. Their forms cast shadows over the furniture; Gabe moved carefully into the unfamiliar space. With the light from the kitchen behind them and beams from the streetlamp outside filtering through the half-open blinds on the front window, he could almost see. The room appeared empty, but anyone could be hiding in the dark corners. He was about to ask Brinna where the nearest light switch was when a piercing shriek shattered the quiet.

He jumped back, but the floor moved beneath his foot, and he felt a slashing pain in his leg. He reached out quickly, shoving Brinna behind him and protecting her from the unknown assailant. They were definitely not alone. His other hand went instinctively to his sidearm.

"Stay back!" he warned her, but she ignored him.

She'd already pushed him to the side, flipped on the light switch, and waltzed right into the room. A potted plant lay on the floor, dirt scattered around. He scanned the room, peered behind the couch, and noted there was no other hiding place large enough to conceal a full-size human. So who in the world had attacked him?

Brinna marched over to an old upright piano and stooped beside it. She scooped something into her arms and whirled to face him.

"You stepped on my cat."

She was, indeed, holding a huge tabby cat.

"Your *cat*?"

"Miss Mimi," she said, smoothing the cat's overly fluffed fur. "She's only got three legs, so she doesn't always move too fast. It makes her a little bit clumsy. She must've knocked the plant over. That's probably the crash we heard from outside."

"Miss Mimi did all that? Well, I didn't mean to step on her. Is she okay?"

"I think so. But I'm afraid you're not her favorite person right now."

From the way the cat glared at him and twitched that heavy tuft of tail, he didn't need to be told they weren't on the way to becoming best friends.

"In my defense," he said, "it was still pretty dark in here. I honestly didn't see her."

"She's a cat. She can see in the dark. I guess she figured you could, too."

"Well, now she knows better. So when did you get a cat?"

"When I got the house," she said, depositing the cat back on the floor. "She came with it."

"I hope you didn't pay extra. It looks like Miss Mimi has seen better days."

The cat was missing a back leg, but there was nothing wrong with her front legs. The stinging pain in Gabe's own leg was proof of that, and he bent to pull up his pant leg and inspect the damage.

"Ouch! Did she do that to you?" Brinna asked when the bright red scratch on his shin became visible.

"Yeah, even missing a limb she's practically lethal. Somehow she managed to go for my good leg, so I'm going to say things are even between me and Miss Mimi."

"You'd better let me wash that and put something on it," Brinna suggested, motioning for him to head back to the kitchen.

"What about the Peeping Tom? We should maybe look over the rest of the house to be sure that—"

"If some stranger had been in here, Miss Mimi wouldn't have been out in the open. She'd have been hiding. I think it's safe to say we're alone."

"She wasn't exactly hiding when I stepped on her."

"Because you were with me," Brinna explained. "She'd have made herself scarce if someone had come in here without me. Come on, sit down and let's get that cleaned up."

He took a seat in one of the kitchen chairs. Miss Mimi followed Brinna as if nothing had happened, hopping along after her, making soft thumping sounds with her huge fuzzy paws. She really was a big cat. How had Gabe not even seen her? Well, he'd been looking for something a little bit larger than a cat, hadn't he?

Brinna opened a cupboard and pulled out a first aid kit. She got warm water from the tap and gave Gabe a cloth so he could wash the wound while she produced a tube of antiseptic cream and a package of bandages. He felt a little foolish. The cat had barely scratched him, so he shouldn't let Brinna make such a big deal of it. He'd certainly been through a lot worse. Then again, how could he say no to her? She was tending to him as if she actually cared. He didn't *want* to say no.

He wanted to say *something*, though. The obvious topic would be to finally tell her how truly sorry he was for what he did. He'd dreamed of apologizing to her for years, but what if she admitted she was better off without him? That her life improved after he left? He wasn't up for that. He'd better say something safer.

"You've got a really nice house," he blurted.

Her smile showed her evident pride. "Thanks. I've made a few updates, but mostly I liked it the way it was when I bought it from Helen Culberson two years ago."

"I remember her. She taught piano, right?"

"Yes, for years and years. She's in assisted living now, but she gave me a good deal on the house. It came with the cat, and she let me keep her piano."

He had to chuckle at that. Brinna seemed to make friends everywhere she went. People recognized her for what she was—gracious, helpful, intelligent, and decent. Mrs. Culberson had obviously known her piano and her cat would be in good hands with Brinna.

"How is that?" Brinna asked as she finished up with the bandage.

"Better than the VA Hospital," he said with a chuckle. "Miss Mimi looks like she survived the ordeal, too."

The cat was oblivious to them, grooming herself on the mat in front of the door.

"Like I said, she'd let us know if there was anything wrong here. I guess the guy outside was just that, some guy outside."

"There've been too many unexplained things for my comfort," he said. "You had a car following you out of town, then you found someone prowling around the old factory. Now you come home and there's a shadowy person in your front yard, and don't forget that thing at the library," he added.

"What thing at the library?" she asked.

"I know you don't believe me, but when we came back to the microfilm readers, mine really was set at a different article. I didn't bump it."

She nodded, considering his words. "Someone was looking at your research while we were in the workroom for a few minutes? But what could they expect to find in such a short time? We were at it for ages and didn't turn up solid information."

"Maybe they knew what they were looking for."

She pondered a moment before asking, "When you looked at your reader again, what sort of article was it set to? Anything about the Boyston scandal?"

He thought about it and then shook his head.

"No, I didn't see any connection. It was a report on some local football game. I know you think I'm imagining it, but—"

"I believe you, Gabe," she assured him. "If you say you didn't bump it, then someone else did. But what could they have been looking for on that microfilm?"

"Maybe they weren't looking at the microfilm. You said yourself it was easy to bump the machine. Maybe they were in the room looking at something else."

She nodded, but her brows drew together. "What else was there to look at? It's a museum. All the stuff on display is for everyone. There's nothing for anyone to sneak around for."

"You didn't have any documents or anything sitting out?"

"No, just that list I made of people involved at the time."

Her eyes grew wide, and she met his gaze. They both realized how someone could be interested in that.

"That list would be exactly the sort of thing someone might want to look at," Gabe said.

"And they could quickly snap a photo of it, just like you did," she added.

"And then they would know just about as much as we do," he said.

"Unless they already know something we don't."

"Which would mean they might have reason to try to stop us investigating. You still think the guy at your front window was just looking for a missing pet?"

"No. That really *would* be too much of a co-incidence."

He could see the fear play in her eyes, and he felt bad for bringing it all up. He wanted her to be careful, but he certainly didn't want her to be afraid.

"Well, I guess we scared him off," he said, hoping to alleviate her worry. "He won't be coming back here."

"I hope that's true. What could he be looking for?"

"I guess that depends on what he knows...or what he thinks we know."

"We don't know anything. I feel like the whole day has been wasted."

"Well, I don't. I wasn't convinced there really was a murder to investigate. Now I'm convinced there was."

"But it was so long ago. Who else would even know about it?"

"The murderer."

"Well, unless he was a serious juvenile at the

time, the guy I saw at my window was way too young."

"I thought you didn't get a good look at him?"

"I didn't, but I saw him move. He didn't move like someone old enough to have committed murder fifty years ago."

Gabe thought about this. Yes, she had a good point. The murderer would have to be in their late sixties, at least. The shadow he saw tonight had to have belonged to a much younger man. If only Mr. Kleinert had been willing to give him some details.

He should have pressed the man, despite his vulnerable state. If Gabe had believed him, perhaps he would've insisted on more information. The truth was, he hadn't believed him. Now he did. At least, he was taking the man's story more seriously.

"So the person who made that confession must be up there in age, too," Brinna commented.

"Yep, they are. I wish I'd asked a few more questions. I will tomorrow."

"You'll talk to your person again?"

"Yes. I'll get some answers, or at least some more clues on what we're looking for."

"I thought we were looking for a missing person."

"We're looking for the whole case." He laughed. "I don't have a suspect. I don't have a motive… I don't even have a body. All I have is a very confused confession and some things I can't explain. Speaking of which…just for my peace of mind, could I take a look through your house? I'm sure that broken pot was just the cat, but I'd feel a lot better if I take a look around."

She gave a frustrated sigh. "Fine, go be a cop. In the meanwhile, I'm making some tea."

She'd always been a tea drinker, and he was glad to see that hadn't changed. He wanted more than anything to sit here at her table drinking tea and hashing over their day.

First, though, he wanted to make sure she was safe. Leaving the kitchen, he found his way through the rest of the house. It wasn't large, just the main rooms downstairs and three bedrooms upstairs. In each room, he saw touches of Brinna. There were colors he knew she liked, antiques she'd collected, shelves lined with books and trinkets that had probably come to her as gifts from loved ones. He felt like an intruder and was thankful when his search turned up nothing suspicious. She had made a cozy home for herself, and he realized he was hopelessly out of place here.

Returning to the kitchen, he announced his findings. "All clear. It's getting late, so I should probably head home. My dad's going to be looking for me."

"Okay, sure. It's good that you can be here for him."

She didn't look up from the kettle. He wished he knew if it was because she was preoccupied with getting the water temperature just right, or if she was a little bit disappointed to see him go. He moved toward the door. Miss Mimi saw him coming and jumped off the mat, hopping her way over to sit by Brinna's feet.

"I'll see you at the library tomorrow," he said, half wishing she'd tell him to stay a while longer.

She nodded and finally turned to face him with a friendly smile. "Absolutely. I'll be there all day."

"Good. Great. I'll text you before I come over."

"Sounds good."

They stood there, doing their best to look like old friends who'd had a chat but didn't care if they waited another ten years before seeing each other again. He believed she might really feel that way, but she could probably read the truth all over his face. The hours they'd spent together today were the best he'd had in a long time.

Gabe put his hand on the doorknob. "You aren't worried about that guy we saw, are you? I could call it in and get someone to keep an eye on things here."

"No, I'm not worried. You checked it out, right? There's nothing to call in and report."

"If you're sure?"

"I am. I've got Miss Slasher to protect me," she said.

He could hardly argue with that, so he smiled and let himself out. She was still watching him when he turned back for one last look. The air outside was cold and damp after sitting with Brinna in her lacy kitchen. Seeing her there only made it harder to leave.

He exhaled a long, heavy breath as he pulled the door shut behind him and headed out to his car. The street was quiet, the front yard was empty, and everything seemed just as it should be. Except that it wasn't. Brinna was living a wonderful life, and Gabe wasn't a part of it.

He'd thought he was ready to come home. He'd thought he was over her. It had never dawned on him that he was still hopelessly in love.

SEVEN

Brinna locked the door behind Gabe and pushed the curtain aside to peer out the window. He reached his car and glanced back up at the house. She waved but wasn't sure if he saw her. She stayed there until he drove away.

Had she really just spent nearly the entire day with Gabe Elliot? She still wasn't sure she could believe that. The very idea was ridiculous. It had taken her years to work through her hurt, anger, and the betrayal she'd felt when he left her. How could she forget all that and enjoy spending time with him?

Well, this had been a very different Gabe than the one she'd pledged to marry, that was for sure. This Gabe didn't have as much to prove as the old Gabe had. She remembered him being quick to argue small points and never being able to acknowledge a need for help of any sort. He'd been a bit of a show-off, too. So far, this version of Gabe was the opposite of that.

It wasn't as if Gabe had been a total jerk. He'd always been kind, and she'd felt completely safe with him. He'd just overshadowed her, and she'd suspected he liked it that way. To be honest, *she* had liked it that way years ago. If Gabe was the outgoing, outspoken one, she never had to measure up to anyone's expectations. If Gabe was bold about his faith, she could simply sit back and agree. She could fade into the background and just be...present. It had been comfortable to let Gabe decide where they'd go on their dates, who they'd hang out with, and what they'd watch on TV. Since he was such a good guy, she was happy to let him lead. In everything.

Then he'd led her to heartbreak.

She hadn't known what to do. At first, she didn't even know what emotion to feel. Sadness? Surprise? Fear? Loneliness? She was twenty years old with a dead-end job, no plans for a future, and no idea who she was. It took a lot of soul-searching to realize she felt all those things...and more.

Now here she was, suddenly worried that Tidal Wave Gabe would capsize her again. Just a few hours in his presence, and she didn't recognize her emotions. She wanted to believe these warm feelings toward Gabe were just shadows of nostalgia, but that didn't quite fit. Sure, his return brought back a lot of fond memories from her youth, but her feelings tonight hadn't been about the past. She'd felt safe, comfortable, and even hopeful with Gabe. That was unexpected…and unwelcome.

What would she do if she found herself watching the clock tomorrow, eagerly waiting for him to text her and say he was heading over to do more research? She wasn't ready to become that girl again, the one who sat around waiting for Gabe, looking to him to brighten her days. She made up her mind right then that she was going to focus on clearing her grandfather's name and nothing else. She wouldn't be tempted by the new-and-improved Gabe Elliot.

She was rescued from her worrisome thoughts by her cell phone buzzing. Her first thought was perhaps Gabe had forgotten something, but she sighed when she saw it was Zoey. It was a sigh of relief, she decided, rather than disappointment.

"Hey, Zoey. What's up?"

"Well, don't you sound chipper," Zoey said, sounding a bit chipper herself. "Is that because you spent all afternoon with Gabe Elliot?"

"What? No, who told you I did that?"

"Dale from the library. Ben saw him at the gas station after work, and he mentioned that you're helping Gabe with some research."

"Wow, word really does get around in a small town."

"So what is he researching? Or is that just some excuse he made up to force you to spend time with him?"

"It's a police thing," Brinna said, intentionally vague. "He wanted some information from the archives."

"Uh-huh, sure. Police do that all the time. What's he researching that he needs so much help from you?"

"I don't think I'm allowed to talk about it," Brinna replied. "Is that why you called me? Just to harass me about Gabe?"

"No, not entirely. I wanted to thank you for going to the hospital with me today. I just got a call from my aunt. She said the last round of blood work on Grandpa wasn't good. He's been on all kinds of antibiotics, but they just aren't taking care of the infection. That cancer ruined his resistance."

"Oh, I'm so sorry, Zoey. It was hard to see him so weak today. He was always the life of the party. How are you coping with it?"

"I'm sad and worried about him." Zoey sighed. Her grandfather was a pillar, not just in their family, but in the community. He meant a lot to Zoey. "I was hoping he'd get better, that he'd be at our wedding. I guess that was just wishful thinking."

"Did your aunt tell you what the next steps are to help him?"

"I don't think anyone knows what else they can do for him. He's old, his body is worn out, and the disease has taken a toll. The doctors say he's in God's hands now. They're not giving us a lot of hope."

"Well, you know your grandfather is a man of faith. If he's in God's hands, that's exactly where he'd want to be, whatever happens."

"I know. I feel so bad for him, though. Some of the things he said to me today…"

"He did apologize a lot, poor guy. Must not like people making a fuss for him."

"That's Grandpa…but there was one thing he said that bothered me after you stepped out of the room."

Brinna tried to remember the specifics of their hospital visit. "When I took the call from my office?"

"Yeah. He was tired, and I was saying goodbye so he could get some sleep, but he grabbed my hand and wouldn't let me go. He seemed emotional about something. He was even crying. He tried to tell me something, but I couldn't make any sense out of it."

"What did he say?"

"He rambled about forgiveness and family. Mostly, he kept saying he's sorry. It broke my heart, Brin."

"Of course it did. I could see you were upset

after we visited. Is there anything I can do for you?"

"No, I'm afraid listening to me whine about it is all you can do."

"How about if I pray with you? That's something I can do."

"Yeah, that would be nice."

Right there at her kitchen table, with her own soul still troubled by events of the day, Brinna took a deep breath and closed her eyes. She pushed the clutter of worry and confusion out of the way and let her mind focus on the simple knowledge that God was listening. No matter what she and Zoey were going through, He was always there for them, inviting them into His presence and offering them peace. She took a slow breath and spoke a prayer for them both.

"Heavenly Father, I pray for my dear friend tonight," she began. "Her grandfather isn't doing too well, and You know his struggles. Zoey is hurting to see him like this. He's been a good man, and she loves him a lot. Let her rest in the comfort of knowing her grandfather is truly in Your hands, and we pray his suffering will ease. Bring healing, if it is Your will, and give the medical staff wisdom to care for him. Mostly, Lord, I pray Zoey will feel Your peace resting on her tonight. Give her assurance that she's not alone and You are looking after her grandfather. Thank

You for such a wonderful friend, Lord. We pray in Your name, Amen."

There was silence at the other end of the line. Finally, she heard Zoey exhale.

"Thanks, Brinna. I needed that. I've been so busy, so caught up in everything… I guess I forgot I don't have to handle everything on my own."

"No, you don't. Remember all those times you prayed with me when I was having such a hard time? Well, I've never forgotten. My faith was pretty low for a while, and I'll always be thankful you were there for me, and you kept bringing me back to God."

"He did all the work." Zoey chuckled. "I was just being your friend."

"Well, I'm thankful for that," Brinna assured her. "And as your friend, I insist you make yourself a cup of tea and get to bed early tonight. You've been running nonstop for weeks now."

"I know, but there's so much to do with work and with Grandpa sick so close to the wedding… But you're right. I need to take a step back and relax. Ben tells me the same thing, although he's got no room to talk. Do you know how much overtime he's put in lately?"

"They keep him pretty busy," Brinna agreed. "He's hoping all his hard work will pay off and he'll be in line for a big promotion once Shirley retires."

Brinna's family wasn't thrilled when her brother went to work for the company that had caused so much trouble for them years ago, but Carolyn Boyston had been CEO then, and she'd taken Ben under her wing, just as she'd done for Brinna. It had seemed like it was her way of trying to make up for what had happened. When Carolyn passed away and her daughter, Shirley Boyston-Jones, took over, Ben became her right-hand man.

Brinna always admired her brother's ambition, but lately, she worried he might regret his tireless commitment. He'd be married soon, and Zoey wasn't going to be happy with Ben's long hours and Shirley's over-reliance on him.

"Will Shirley ever retire?" Zoey joked. "She's got to be seventy now and still going strong. I keep telling Ben he needs to be careful about his expectations. No matter how hard he works, he's not a Boyston. We all know Shirley's son, Drexel, is going to be the next CEO."

Brinna couldn't argue with that. Drexel Boyston-Jones had to be almost fifty years old himself by now. He'd been in his mother's shadow his whole life, and his grandmother's shadow before that. The Boyston women had done wonders to build the business, but not much to mold Drexel into a good businessman. He'd get the promotion, but Ben would do all the work.

"Maybe Ben's right and Drexel won't want to be CEO. For now, you need to take care of yourself," Brinna said, trying to change the subject. "Think about something more positive."

"You mean like you and Gabe Elliot being all buddy-buddy again?"

Oh, great. Brinna should have known they'd eventually get back onto that subject.

"We are not buddies," she quickly corrected. "He asked for my help in a professional capacity, that's all. We're both adults now, and the past is the past."

"It didn't seem that way when he was giving you that famous Gabe smile earlier today. Come on, Brin. Distract me from my troubles and give me the juicy details. What did the two of you talk about?"

"It's a police investigation," Brinna reminded her. "We talked about that, and he wouldn't give me the juicy details, so I don't have any to give you."

"How long did you work with him?"

"A couple hours."

"You really spent a couple hours with Gabe Elliot and didn't come to blows? So…did he apologize for what he did to you?"

"No, not in so many words."

"But you're willing to forgive him anyway?"

"I forgave him years ago. We've moved on."

"Wow. Impressive adult behavior."

"Because we *are* adults. I asked about his service, and he said I have a nice house."

She heard Zoey audibly choke. "He saw your *house*? When was he at your house?"

Brinna winced. She hadn't meant to mention that. Zoey would never let it go without an explanation. There was nothing she could do but fill her in on what had taken place tonight. Her surprise was understandable.

"I can't believe you weren't going to tell me all this. Someone followed you…then there was a prowler at your house?"

"I wasn't going to tell you this because it's probably nothing, and I don't want you to make a big deal out of it," Brinna explained.

"You're spooked because you think this has something to do with whatever Gabe is researching," Zoey noted. "Just what sort of investigation is this, anyway?"

"I can't tell you about it," Brinna reminded her. "I'm helping Gabe again tomorrow, and we'll know more after that. It might be a bunch of nothing, so there's no point in getting worked up. Okay?"

"If you say so. What did he think about your cat?"

"Let's just say their first meeting didn't exactly go well."

Brinna recounted the story of Gabe stepping on Miss Mimi, and Zoey laughed. It was good to bring the conversation back around to something light. Brinna was finally able to leave it at that, knowing her friend felt more at ease over her own troubles and reassured that things were in a good place between Brinna and Gabe.

"Now get some rest and don't worry about anything," Brinna said, stifling a yawn.

"All right, and the same goes for you," Zoey replied. "Let me know how things go with Gabe tomorrow. I know you say it's all very amicable and platonic now, but you can't blame me for hoping. If things are so cool between you, my big dilemma is solved."

"Your dilemma?"

"For the seating chart at my wedding reception. Now I don't have to figure out how to keep you guys at opposite ends of the room."

Brinna laughed. "Good night, Zoey."

Zoey was still chuckling when they hung up. Brinna shook her head but smiled. She really was thankful to have a good friend like Zoey. God knew what He was doing when He brought the rich girl from the other side of town and Brinna together. Sometimes it seemed like they had nothing in common, but they'd been friends for so long that Brinna couldn't imagine her life without Zoey. And now they were going to be sisters.

It really was a blessing.

She stood and stretched her tired muscles. Miss Mimi meowed and hugged her legs. Brinna stooped to scratch her ears.

"Okay, clumsy cat. Let's go clean up that plant you knocked over and head up to bed."

She wasn't sure how well she'd sleep after a day like today, despite her exhaustion. She'd insisted she was fine, that her fears had been unfounded, but were they really? If someone was following her around, that meant someone else knew about Gabe's investigation. Who else knew about it though, except the person who had confessed?

Maybe she should ponder that a bit more. Who was it? They must be fairly elderly now. That narrowed the field. And Gabe had indicated the person had confessed to him in his capacity as a minister.

Okay, that could be anyone in their seventies or eighties, or even older. But Gabe worried this person might not be in their right mind. Could it be someone he'd visit as a shut-in, or in a nursing home, or…in the hospital?

Brinna practically tripped over her own feet as she walked into the living room.

Of course. Why hadn't she thought of it sooner?

She'd run into Gabe at the hospital, where he'd been doing visitations. That's when he first mentioned the investigation. It would've been someone he'd visited that morning. Who had he'd seen? The only one she knew of was...

No, it couldn't be. Could it?

She didn't want to believe it, but it made perfect sense. She should have figured it out right away, in fact. No wonder Gabe was being so tight-lipped about it. He didn't want to believe it himself, and for good reason.

The person who'd confessed had to be Zoey's grandfather—dear, sweet, faithful Mr. Kleinert himself. How could he possibly have been involved in a murder?

EIGHT

Gabe tried not to be too eager to meet Brinna at the library the next morning. He went about his day as usual—making sure his father ate a decent breakfast, checking in for the first shift staff meeting at the station, and then catching up on emails and paperwork in his office. By ten o'clock, he couldn't sit at his desk any longer. He paced the floor while he texted Brinna.

Thankfully, she replied right away. Yes, she was in her office, and yes, now was as good a time as any for him to come over and get back to their research. He practically whooped with enthusiasm as he gathered his things and let dispatch know where he'd be. Hopefully, they'd find something today that would confirm whether to initiate a formal investigation or to drop it entirely. It would be great to be out from under the uncertainty, but he wasn't thrilled about losing a good excuse to spend time with Brinna.

Sure, he'd see her around town, and of course,

she couldn't avoid him at her brother's wedding. Those situations wouldn't be the same as working together, though. She'd been polite toward him, but he was pretty sure she wasn't ready to make space for him on her social calendar.

That was all the more reason to enjoy their research time today. He waved at the front-desk librarian when he entered the building. She smiled and nodded her head toward the hallway to the Historical Society wing. Obviously, word was out that he and Brinna were working on a project together.

The museum section was empty, so he went through to the work area where Brinna's office was. Her door was open, and she sat at her desk, studying her computer screen. Her trusty notebook was at her side, and she was scribbling in it. She seemed so engrossed in her work that he almost hated to interrupt.

"I see you started without me," he said, knocking at her doorframe.

She glanced up. "And I think I've found something, too."

"May I come in?"

"Of course."

She motioned toward a nearby chair, so he pulled it up beside her and peered over to see her notes. She held the notebook out for him to read more easily.

"Here, look at this name. Have you seen it before?"

There were several names jotted down on the page, but she pointed to one in particular. She'd underlined it and marked it with a star.

"Barty Swenson?"

"Does that ring any bells?" she asked.

"No, I don't think so. Should it?"

"Maybe not, but he was involved with the big factory project fifty years ago."

"Swenson? Hmm, I don't know anyone around here with that name. He worked for Boyston?"

"He was some kind of investor," she replied, leaning in to study her computer. "He wasn't one of the Boyston employees, so that's probably why we didn't see his name pop up in the articles we were searching."

"So where did you find him?"

"In an article from six months before the scandal. It didn't seem like we were getting anywhere just scrolling through newspapers looking for headlines, so I decided to go to the computer and search the name of our prime suspect. That eventually led me to this earlier article, so I just—"

"Wait…our prime suspect? I didn't realize we had one."

"Of course we do. The person who confessed the murder to begin with."

"But I didn't... How did you search for their name when I haven't told you who it was?"

She peered up at him with a slightly annoyed look on her face. "Come on, Gabe, I'm not that obtuse. You practically admitted the confession came from someone you visited as hospital chaplain, and we both know it has to be someone at least seventy years old who also has connections with Boyston Industries. It was pretty easy to narrow that down. I looked up Zoey's grandfather and found this article."

He was impressed with her reasoning, of course, but also frustrated with himself. He shouldn't have been so transparent. The whole point of not reporting the man's confession right away was to protect him from others finding out, just in case it was simply a delusion. He never meant for Brinna to know about Mr. Kleinert's involvement, at least not until he might have to go public with it.

Now that she'd figured it out, he couldn't very well deny it. He wasn't ready to confirm it, though. He still owed that to the old man.

"I'm going to withhold comment on your deduction...for now," he said. "But I'm compelled to point out that the confession I heard—whoever it came from—was not an actual confession of committing murder, but of being aware that a murder had been committed. Is that understood?"

"Totally. You can neither confirm nor deny anything. But I'm right."

He couldn't help but smile at her confidence. "Let's just look at that article, okay? Why do you think this Swanson person is significant?"

"*Swen*son, Barty Swenson," Brinna corrected. "Here's what I found."

She explained that the article she'd been reading wasn't from the newspaper, but from a now-defunct regional magazine focused on local business. Mr. Kleinert had been interviewed as a representative of Boyston Industries. At the time of the interview, he'd overseen the early phases of the building project. He'd been asked about the planned expansion and what that would mean for the local economy.

The article popped up as a resource material used in a university study done a dozen years ago regarding businesses that had filed for bankruptcy and managed to rebound. If not for that study and the fact that it had been posted online, she never would've found this article. He really had to hand it to Brinna, she knew how to do her research. He'd be wise to never try to hide anything from her again.

Gabe skimmed through the article and paused when he found the name Brinna had singled out. It wasn't much, but the man was influential in the project, or Mr. Kleinert wouldn't have brought him up.

"It says that Clement Boyston promoted the idea of building a second factory for two years before it actually got the go-ahead from the board of directors," he said, condensing as he went along. "Mr. Kleinert was made project manager at the time and was praised for his dedication and youthful enthusiasm. I just wonder why there's no mention of your grandfather. I thought he was the project manager, and that's why all the suspicion landed on him when it went bad."

"He was brought into the project about halfway through it, I believe," Brinna explained. "I don't know any details. I just know there were always hard feelings between him and Mr. Kleinert."

"Yeah, it sounds like he was raring to go for this. He couldn't have been happy to be told to step aside so someone else could take over. Here he says the board gave them the green light on the project when Mr. Boyston brought in Barty Swenson, an investor from the East Coast. He joined the team, and his million-dollar infusion meant they were ready to break ground. Mr. Kleinert said New Minden would never be the same after."

"He was right about that, unfortunately," Brinna noted. "But that's it. That's the only mention of Barty Swenson. When the scandal broke

and the newspapers ran stories about it, there was
no mention of him at all."

"So what happened to Mr. Swenson and his
million-dollar infusion?"

"That's what I'm wondering."

"He definitely seems like a loose thread we
ought to look into."

"I did that," Brinna said with a proud grin.
"Just look at this."

She clicked her computer to open another tab.
"Barty Swenson was declared legally dead in
New Jersey forty-five years ago. In the court fil-
ing, his wife said he left her the very same year
our big scandal happened, and she never saw him
again. After five years, she had him declared legally dead so their son could get the man's life
insurance to save for college."

"Wow. That's some very good detective work,"
Gabe said.

"That's what studying history is," she informed
him. "Following leads, searching for truth. I
never thought I'd be discovering a murder right
here in New Minden, though. It does kind of
seem like what Mr. Kleinert told you was true,
doesn't it?"

"Yes, I'm afraid it does. Not that I'm confirming it *was* Mr. Kleinert who told me."

"No, of course not." She laughed and then pre-
tended to shush herself. "So what's the next step?"

"I'm afraid I have a decision to make," he said and exhaled slowly as the seriousness of the situation began to dawn on him. "Do I pretend none of this ever happened? Or do I take it to my chief and start an official investigation, accepting all that will entail?"

Brinna's cheerful smile faded. "You mean, digging up all the old dirt around the Boyston scandal. You'll drag my grandfather through the mud all over again because of this."

"So far, there's no reason to think your grandfather has any connection to it," he assured her.

"But there's a connection to Boyston Industries," she pointed out sharply. "That will be more than enough to make people doubt him again. He'll be devastated."

"Not to mention what it will do to the poor old soul who actually made the confession to begin with," Gabe noted. "This investigation will open a can of worms for a lot of good people, Brinna."

"But you can't just ignore everything we've found, can you?"

He shook his head. "No, I'm afraid I can't. My chief will probably want an investigator to talk to your grandfather, and we'll need to get an official statement from the person who confessed. None of this will be easy."

"Are you sure about this, Gabe? Are you sure

we've found enough information to make all of this really necessary?"

Her eyes practically begged him. More than anything, he would love to reassure her, to tell her there wouldn't be an investigation. But he couldn't do that. He was spared from having to answer her when her desk phone started ringing.

She looked startled but answered it quickly. From her responses to the person on the other end, Gabe determined it was a call from someone within the library, one of her coworkers. She spoke briefly, then hung up and pushed her chair back from the desk.

"That was Dale, our reference librarian," she said. "Someone at his desk needs my help. Apparently, he's a writer from out of town doing some research."

This was a welcome interruption.

"A writer? What's he researching?"

Brinna's brows wrinkled, and she seemed perplexed. "Passenger railways through small towns in Ohio. Apparently, he heard about the New Minden Station collection."

"What's that?"

"When the train station shut down here in town, they donated all their old records and documents to the Historical Society. We've got schedules, maps, ticketing information, all sorts of stuff."

"You mean, passenger trains came through here?" Gabe asked.

Brinna nodded. "They did. My grandparents talk about how they used to get a ticket and go down to Columbus for the day, or all the way up to Sandusky on Lake Erie. They could stop off at any of the little towns along the way and visit friends or do some shopping."

"I had no idea. Sounds like this guy came to the right place."

"Yeah, but it's kind of funny…"

"In what way?"

"Dale says this man is especially interested in information from the time period about three years before the trains stopped running through here. Want to guess when that was?"

Gabe didn't have to guess. He could tell just by the concerned look on Brinna's face.

"Um, was it right around fifty years ago?"

She nodded. "Yep."

He pushed his chair back and stood so she could easily get past him. "Well, then. Mind if I follow you out? I'd like to get a look at this out-of-town writer who has a sudden interest in New Minden fifty years ago."

Brinna left her office and headed out through the collection room into the main area of the library. Gabe followed. Dale was talking with a middle-aged man at the reference desk. Gabe stopped her by putting his hand on her elbow. He spoke softly so only she could hear him.

"I think I'd rather observe from afar. If this guy is here to investigate the same things we are, he might not appreciate the uniform. Don't mention what I was doing here, okay?"

"Sure, okay," she agreed.

Gabe let her continue, and he lingered at a book display near the front entrance. She noticed him pick up a book about knitting and pretend to study it. She hoped that wouldn't look suspicious to anyone.

Dale smiled as she approached. "Here's Brinna Jenson now."

"Hi," Brinna greeted the man, holding out her hand to him. "I'm the archivist historian here. Dale says you're interested in our collection of materials from the railroad?"

The man introduced himself as he shook her hand. "Pete Snare. Yes, I'm working on a book about passenger rail in Ohio, and Dale says you have a good collection. Sorry I didn't call first, but I just got into town and thought I'd take the chance someone might be available to help me."

"I'm happy to show you what we have. Where are you from, Mr. Snare?"

"Oh, I've been researching all through Ohio for the past couple weeks. I have to say, I was surprised when Dale explained you have a whole wing here dedicated to local history. That seems…unusual for such a small town."

"We had a very generous donor who cared a lot about the history of our area and education," she explained briefly, nodding to Dale as he turned away to help another patron. "Come on, I'll take you to the collection room."

Brinna made eye contact with Gabe as she led Mr. Snare past him on the way to the archival area. Gabe was still perusing his knitting book, but she knew his full focus was on Pete Snare. She hadn't missed the fact that Mr. Snare hadn't quite answered her question about where he was from. For Gabe's sake, she decided to ask again.

"So you've been all through Ohio on this project," she said casually. "Where is your home base?"

"I've been working out of Chicago lately," he said as they entered the historical wing of the building. He paused at the wide doorway, reading the name posted above. "The Carolyn Boyston History Center. Well, that sounds very impressive. Is that named after the generous benefactor you mentioned?"

"Yes," Brinna replied. "Mrs. Boyston's family has been very influential in New Minden and our county for generations. When she passed away several years ago, this was her gift to the community."

Pete followed her into the collections room. He sauntered from one display to another, studying it all with much greater interest than Brinna would've expected. He seemed less interested in the actual artifacts than in the way they were presented.

"This is quite well done," he commented. "The framing on this old map is amazing."

"That's the first plat of New Minden," she explained. "A local carpenter crafted the actual frame for us, and the document is preserved behind UV protected glass. Are you familiar with archival preservation?"

"Oh, only in that I've seen some good examples and some not so good," he replied. "Your setup here seems to be very state-of-the-art. This Boyston lady must've really had some big bucks to leave you."

Brinna could still see Gabe through the doorway and down the hall. He wasn't looking at her, and she tried not to blatantly stare at him. Could he still hear their conversation? No, probably not. It made Brinna uncomfortable to discuss finances with this stranger, but as a public institution, the library had a duty to be as transparent as possible about its use of funding.

Ordinarily, it wouldn't have bothered Brinna

in the least to explain how careful they were to keep the library budget well in hand, to use their resources wisely in service to their patrons and the community. Right now, she felt a bit awkward. The way Mr. Snare seemed to be evaluating everything was a bit off-putting.

"The Boyston family has done well in business over multiple generations," she said, making a beeline for the cabinet that held the collection from the old rail depot. "Here's where we keep the items donated to us when the local train depot shut down. What are you most interested in?"

"Oh, um…let's start with schedules. Do you have copies of the schedules for passenger trains?"

"I believe so," she said, pulling open a drawer and glancing through the contents.

She couldn't see Gabe from this side of the room, but she wanted to think he was lingering near the front desk, still flipping pages in that knitting book. There was nothing threatening about Pete Snare, but Brinna just didn't feel… settled.

Maybe she was imagining things. He seemed grateful when she found a large binder with several years' worth of train schedules gathered in it. She laid the book out on a table and stepped back to let him begin looking through it.

"This contains schedules from the last years

of operation," she said as she went back to the drawer. "What years are you most interested in?"

"Oh, this should be good," he answered.

As Dale had mentioned over the phone, it seemed the man really was interested in the time period that corresponded with the Boyston scandal and the possible murder. Could that just be a coincidence? Or was Pete Snare looking for more than just information about Ohio's rail history?

He flipped through the binder and took a couple of photos of some pages. That certainly wasn't out of the ordinary. He'd surely want to refer to these again as his book progressed…if there really was a book.

"So, can you tell me anything about the accuracy of these old schedules?" he asked after a few moments. "I mean, did the trains run on time? Did they only stop at the places listed here, or could they make unscheduled stops along the way?"

She shook her head. "Sorry, that was all before my time. I'm afraid I don't know about that."

He chuckled. "Wish I could say it was before my time. I was young back then, but I was around while these trains were still running."

"And did you ever travel on them?"

"No, I never rode on these old lines. It's just not the same now with highways and interstates."

"I guess that's why you're writing about it, to capture that era and keep the memories alive."

"Yeah, something like that. So, you wouldn't have information about changes to the schedules, would you? Did they post daily updates when a train wasn't running or when an extra stop was added?"

She thought about that for a moment. "Hmm, I don't recall seeing anything like that, but we can look at some of the sales registers to see if they might contain information about schedule changes."

"Sales registers?"

She pulled open another drawer. "The station masters kept very detailed registers of ticket sales. We can see who bought tickets, when they were purchased, and where they were going. It's pretty amazing."

"You have all of that information?"

"Haven't you run across registers like this in any of the other places you've been researching? I'm told the railroads were sticklers for keeping detailed records. Here, they were kept in these binders—"

"Brinna?" one of her coworkers called to her from the doorway. "There's a call for you. It sounds pretty important."

Brinna excused herself from Mr. Snare, but he hardly seemed to notice. His eyes had gone big and round at the sight of the binders containing the ticket registers. Brinna knew the feeling. There was nothing quite like stumbling upon some hidden gems while doing research.

Brinna ducked into her office and picked up the call. It was Zoey.

"It's my grandpa," she said quickly, sounding upset. "He had a bad night, and he's not doing well today."

"Oh, I'm so sorry, Zoey. Are you at the hospital with him?"

"Yes, but I don't think he's aware of us. It's really hard, Brinna. I'm just not ready for this. He's lapsed into a coma, and the doctors don't know if he'll ever wake up."

Brinna's heart sank for her friend. This was not the news any of them wanted. Gabe had plans to ask the older man for more information. Zoey planned for her grandfather to be at her wedding. Sadly, it seemed their plans were about to change.

NINE

The next three days brought more changes than expected. Mr. Kleinert passed away peacefully on Friday night. With his family surrounding him, he slipped away and never regained consciousness. The family contacted Gabe and thanked him for giving their loved one such comfort at the end. Gabe prayed with them and encouraged them to contact his father to start planning the funeral. Thankfully, they did.

Then on Saturday morning when Gabe met with his chief to explain that Mr. Kleinert had confessed to covering up a murder, Gabe felt like a heel. It was the right thing to do, of course, but he couldn't feel good about it. When faced with Gabe's findings, though, Chief Siegle agreed that a report needed to be filed and an investigation opened. He put Gabe in charge of it. At first Gabe worried that his coworkers would feel he was stepping on their toes. He soon found out they were glad to stay clear of it—no one wanted to be a part of this investigation.

Chief Siegle assured Gabe that he'd get all the support he needed. In fact, the chief decided that the best way to get on top of the rumors that would soon be blazing through town was to contact the Kleinert family and inform them of the investigation. As Gabe expected, that did not go very well. The family took it as a betrayal. How dare Gabe take on this investigation! He was a fool if he thought for one minute their dear patriarch could have been involved in anything like murder. Ben was angry at Gabe for upsetting Zoey, and Zoey was upset with Brinna for working with Gabe.

It was quite a slap in the face, actually. It especially stung because Gabe hated being the cause of a rift between Brinna and Zoey. That certainly hadn't been expected and he regretted it greatly.

Gabe's father managed to avoid the Kleinert family's ire. Due to his previous good relationship with the deceased, he was honored to serve with funeral preparations. Gabe did what he could to help his father, but it was clear the family did not want him involved.

So, he focused on the investigation. Now that he had a name and a possible time line, Gabe contacted the police department in Barty Swenson's hometown in New Jersey. They were able to confirm that Mrs. Swenson did report her husband missing, and the timing lined up perfectly with the scandal at Boyston Industries. It was all just as Brinna had said. The man had come to Ohio to invest in the factory expansion, that project failed miserably, and he apparently never returned home. Nothing was ever said about what happened to his money.

So far, Gabe's investigation had only clarified what they already knew. Brinna's grandfather had been perfectly positioned to embezzle the money. No proof was found to indict him, but no proof was found to let him off the hook, either. The case simply went cold, and the people of New Minden pulled their lives together again.

Now it was Monday afternoon and the people of New Minden pulled together to lay Mr. Kleinert to rest. Their church was filled with mourners. Many came to the funeral to pay their respects to a good man, but a few were there to see if the rumors they heard about a possible murder investigation were true. No one seemed especially interested in Gabe's presence.

Despite it all, Gabe's father provided a beautiful service. He had Kay Hefler and other dedicated church members to make sure everything went smoothly, while Gabe remained in the background. The profusion of altar flowers were placed just right, service bulletins were in order, the music was uplifting, and Dad's sermon gave comfort and inspiration. It all went perfectly.

As the service came to an end, the family members somberly filed out of the sanctuary. The pews behind them emptied next. Gabe had positioned himself near one of the exits to greet people on their way out and although no one was outwardly rude, he could feel the cold glances.

Mostly, though, he was aware of Brinna. She'd been sitting a few rows behind Zoey and Ben, on the other side of the church. He'd avoided making eye contact with her all through the service, but he could feel her approaching him now.

"I hear you're leading the investigation," she said, foregoing any niceties.

"Nobody else wants it," he admitted. "Are you following everyone to the cemetery?"

She shook her head. "No, I'm not really sure I'm wanted there."

"I hope you haven't had too much trouble with...things."

She clearly knew what he meant. "Zoey's furious with me. She thinks I should've told her what her grandfather said to you, and that I shouldn't have helped you. Ben's taking her side, so things are a bit tense right now."

"Sorry about that. Ben called me yesterday and had some strong words. But then he confirmed everything is still on track for the wedding rehearsal in eleven days. And he invited me to the big party Shirley Boyston is throwing for the happy couple on Friday night. Go figure."

She chuckled. "Yeah, Ben is always practical. It's one of his most redeeming qualities. Zoey, however, carries a grudge. I'll be happy if she even speaks to me at that party on Friday. Are you planning to be there?"

"I ought to be there since Ben made the effort to invite me," he replied. "But you might be the only one there who won't give me the cold shoulder. That is…as long as you don't plan to shun me."

"I think we'll be shunned together, unfortunately. It seems Mr. Kleinert was more involved in things during the scandal than we've been led to believe."

"Oh?" he asked.

She glanced around, and he realized this was hardly the place for this discussion. His current social standing could have a negative impact on hers. They'd better keep things quiet regarding the investigation.

"Why don't we meet up again later, after the funeral supper. Want to come by the library? I'm taking most of the day off today, but I'll need to go in and catch up on a few things at some point."

"That sounds good," he replied. "Maybe around four o'clock?"

"Great. My grandfather donated some things

a few months ago. They've just been sitting in a box in the workroom waiting for me to finish sorting them out. I figured now was a good time to dive in."

"What kind of things did he donate?"

"Mostly old photos and papers from his time at Boyston. The timing is great. We might learn a few things there."

"Wow. That could be just what we need to figure out what really went on back then."

"I don't want to get too excited. He said the police went through all this stuff back in the day. I think that's why he kept it all. It was evidence in the case, but once they realized they couldn't charge him, they gave it back. He probably kept it in case the issue ever reared up again."

"Smart man. Maybe we'll see something now that the investigation missed then. At least we've got the name of our missing man to focus on. I wonder what your grandfather remembers about him?"

"I assumed you'd want to talk to him about that. Can I please be with you when you interview him?"

"Sure, if he's okay with that. In light of Mr. Kleinert's passing, I've held off scheduling any interviews, but now that the funeral is done, I'll contact the remaining parties who were involved. Sadly, there aren't too many of them left."

"Fifty years is a long time. Who do you plan to talk to?"

"Well, there's Shirley Boyston-Jones, and a woman named Tammy Crenshaw. She was Mr. Boyston's secretary. Your grandfather had a secretary, but she has since passed away. I believe there was a young factory foreman who was brought onto the project, and I found his contact information. Other than that, I can't think of anyone else who worked closely on the venture. I'm hoping your grandfather might give me some other names of people to talk to."

She shook her head. "I wish I could assure you he'll be cooperative, but this topic will really touch some nerves. I honestly don't know how helpful he'll be. He won't like being interrogated again, that's for sure."

"It's not an interrogation," he assured her. "He's not under arrest or even under suspicion. I just need any information I can get that might help me understand what happened."

"I know. I'm just warning you that he won't be happy with you."

"I'm used to that. For the past few days, it seems like I've upset the whole town…except maybe you, ironically."

"Oh, I'm upset," she said and then gave him a smile. "You haven't called me these last couple days. I'd hoped we could meet up for more research. I'm just as invested in finding the truth as you are, Gabe Elliot."

Her words surprised him and he smiled back at her. He couldn't help but wonder, though, if either of them were really prepared for whatever truth they might find.

Brinna enjoyed the rest of her afternoon. She really had been upset Gabe hadn't included her in the investigation the past few days. She saw how everyone was treating him, and she could only feel sorry for the poor guy. At the funeral lunch, she made sure that he was included in conversation around their table.

As the lunch ended and people gave their well-wishes to the family and went on their way, Gabe busied himself helping his father. He'd assured her they would meet up at four o'clock today, so she gave Zoey a hug and went off to run a couple of errands since she wasn't expected at work.

It was odd to come away from a funeral feeling so hopeful and light. It wasn't the funeral or the mourners who were affecting her attitude. She might as well admit that she felt hopeful and light because Gabe had been happy to see her. His surprised grin when she'd walked up to him after the service was an image she couldn't shake from her mind. Not that she wanted to.

At first, she wasn't sure if she should let herself feel this way, but there was really no point in fighting it. She still enjoyed spending time with Gabe, and she was rapidly growing to like him more and more. This investigation was a wonderful excuse to get to know him again, to find out who he had become and truly allow God to help her heal from her pain. The old trauma was gone, and her anger had evaporated.

She picked up a few groceries and dropped them off at her house. Miss Mimi was happy to see her, so she sat for a few minutes peacefully stroking the cat and making a list of the people Gabe had mentioned he wanted to speak with. He probably had his own list, but she liked lists, and it would be good to have these names handy when they talked to her grandfather. He would've known all these people, and he might remember something interesting about them.

Of course, the name currently at the top of the list was her grandfather, Isaac Randall. Brinna's mother had only been nine years old when the scandal broke, so she wouldn't have inside information to offer them, but perhaps Brinna's grandmother might remember something. It would be good to get her perspective on things, too.

Next on the list was Shirley Boyston-Jones, the current CEO. She would've been a young woman at the time, just getting involved in the family business. Still, she was around during the scandal and would remember things about it. She could also access company records from that time, if she was willing to share them. It would be uncomfortable if Gabe had to procure a court order.

Brinna chewed on her pencil and pondered. It might be a good idea to talk to Shirley's husband, Renner Jones. Brinna couldn't remember if they were married back then, but she'd heard his wealthy family had been close friends with the Boystons. They'd apparently helped rescue Boyston Industries after the scandal. He must know something.

Then there was the secretary Gabe had mentioned, Tammy Crenshaw. She would certainly be someone worth talking to. Mr. Boyston's private secretary would've seen all the paperwork, would've drafted financial statements and typed correspondence. She probably knew as much—or more—than anyone.

Lastly, she added the name of the factory foreman, Bob Afton. From what Gabe had said, he'd been brought onto the project late, so maybe he hadn't been aware of any shady dealings. Gabe said he'd found the man's contact information, so they ought to find out what he knew.

It wasn't a very long list, that was certain.

The police hadn't looked into Barty Swenson back then. Somehow, he'd been ignored by the investigators, probably because he hadn't been around to interview. There must be a reason people hadn't talked about him then. Either he wasn't important, or someone was covering up the fact that he *was*. Obviously, there were still things to learn, and if they just kept digging, they were bound to find them.

She tucked the list in her purse and checked her phone. Three missed calls. Oops, she'd turned it off during the funeral and forgotten to turn it back on. Someone at the library had been trying to contact her. She quickly called them back.

"Sorry to bother you," her coworker Jen said after Brinna apologized for being unavailable. "That guy was in here looking for you again."

"That guy?"

"The writer, Pete something or other."

"Oh, Pete Snare. Yeah, he was in last week doing research. What did he need?"

"I don't know," Jen replied. "I found him trying to get into the history center. He said he was looking for you."

"That's weird. The note on my door said I was out. Was anyone able to help him?"

"No, that was the funny thing. Dale offered to open the center and help him with research, but he declined. He said he'd come back later when you're here and wanted to know when that would be. I told him you wouldn't be back in until tomorrow. I hope that was okay?"

"That's fine. I spent two hours with him on Saturday, so I don't know what he can possibly still want to look at. We went through all the railroad collection."

"He's an odd guy," Jen assessed. "I thought so the very first time I saw him on Thursday."

"You mean Friday," Brinna corrected. "He came on Friday, and Dale sent him back to me."

"Hmm, I remember that, but only because I'd already seen him poking around the periodical room on Thursday. He wasn't reading anything, just looking around. I asked if I could help him find anything, and he said he was looking for old newspapers from fifty years ago. Well, I told him that was all in the history center. I showed him where that was, but he didn't go in. He just stood there looking at the name over the doorway and laughing. He made some joke about New Minden changing its name to New Boyston. It was really strange... Then he chuckled some more and left."

"Are you sure that was on Thursday?" Brinna asked. "He told me he didn't get into town until Friday."

"It was Thursday for sure, because I went to lunch with my boyfriend right after that and told him about it, that's how creeped out I was. Thursday was the only day we had lunch together last week."

"Well, I'm heading in to catch up on a few

things so if he happens to call back, I'll be there to help him," Brinna said.

"Are you sure about that?"

"Yes, I'm sure. He seemed perfectly harmless when I helped him before."

"Okay, then. I'll see you in a bit."

Jen still didn't sound convinced, but Brinna wasn't worried. Pete Snare was slightly odd, as Jen had pointed out, but then again, he was a writer. They couldn't expect him to be totally normal, could they?

She said goodbye to Miss Mimi and headed off. If Gabe was going to come by as he said he would, she needed to hurry. Since the weather was so nice, she wanted to walk. It was just a few blocks to the library, and she'd already done all her errands for the day, so there was no need for her car.

As she arrived, she encountered a young mother struggling with two rambunctious youngsters and a toddler in a stroller. Brinna loved to see parents bringing their children to the library. She dashed ahead to hold the door open for them. The breathless mother thanked her and asked for directions to the children's section. Brinna happily showed them the way.

She stopped by the front desk to let Jen know she'd arrived and was happy to hear there'd been no additional phone calls from Pete Snare. She didn't mind helping people, but she was looking forward to continuing the research with Gabe. They could hardly talk about the investigation with someone hovering over them.

She pulled out her keys and was just about to unlock the main doors to the history center when Gabe came up behind her. She startled and then smiled at him and checked the clock on the wall nearby.

"You're a little bit early," she noted.

"I guess I'm eager to get started," he replied. "Did you just get here?"

"I had some things to do after the funeral. Come on, we can go in and..."

Words failed her as she stepped into the main collection room and discovered a mess. Drawers were pulled open, chairs were knocked over, and documents were scattered everywhere.

She gasped. "What on earth happened?"

Gabe shifted into police mode in an instant. He put a hand on her arm to stop her from entering farther into the room.

"You just unlocked the door, didn't you?" he asked.

"Yes. It's been locked up all day."

"Well, someone got in here," he said. "At a glance, do you see anything missing?"

She scanned the room. Her mind was in a whirl and things were out of place, but she honestly couldn't see anything missing. The really price-less items all seemed to still be in their places. In fact, nothing really looked damaged.

"No...not right off," she replied. "It's almost like someone wanted it to look like the place had been ransacked, but it's just sort of messed up a bit."

"Does any area seem more messed up than another?"

She thought about that for a moment. It was hard to be sure without going into the room and really getting a look at things, but from where she stood now, it appeared the biggest part of the disarray was the quantity of papers strewn around. As she studied them, she realized they were familiar. She'd been looking at them very recently, in fact.

"The papers," she said. "I think those are from that box over there."

"What sort of papers were in that box?"

She swallowed hard and took a deep breath. "That's the box of documents donated by my grandfather. The things the police held as evidence for their initial investigation fifty years ago."

TEN

So much for Brinna's hope for a quiet afternoon doing research with Gabe. Her first instinct was to quickly put things back in order, but he insisted she shouldn't touch anything. Instead, he ushered her back into the library lobby and called his chief, despite Brinna's pleas against it.

"This is a public facility," he told her. "We don't have a choice. It's a police matter whether we like it or not."

She knew he was right, of course, so she waited as patiently as she could for a uniformed officer to arrive. The other library workers whispered among themselves as word got out about the apparent break-in, but Gabe instructed them to carry on with their business as usual. He did a quick walk-through around the rest of the building and determined there was no threat to anyone, so there was no reason to disrupt the rest of the library or its patrons.

Officer Lanford arrived, and Gabe ushered

him back into the history center. Since the main door to the history center had been locked, the first thing he and Lanford did was search for another point of entry. They found it right away. The rear door off the workroom had been pried open. Because the library was open, the alarm system had been turned off. Ordinarily, the main doors to this wing would've been open, and anyone tossing things around in the history center would've been immediately seen. Today, because Brinna had been at the funeral, the trespasser had been hidden behind locked doors.

It was amazing that more damage hadn't been done, actually. Brinna itched to start sorting things, to take inventory and make sure the collection was okay, but Gabe and the officer were busy taking photos and making careful notes about everything. All she could do was follow them around and answer questions about the various items that had been disturbed here and there.

"Does it look like most of these documents on the floor came out of that box from your grandfather?" he asked her.

They were standing over the documents now, and she peered down at them. "Yes, that's where they're from. I know those drawers are open over there, but the documents in that collection are still in there. All the things lying around definitely came from this box."

Gabe consulted with the other officer regarding whether they should try to take fingerprints off things before allowing Brinna to start cleaning up.

"Don't you dare start smearing that black dusty stuff all over these delicate papers," she ordered. "If you need to dust for prints, you can do the box and these chairs over here. You can check the drawer pulls too, but don't do anything that will harm the documents, all right?"

The officer agreed. Gabe called in a request for a detective to come take care of that. Meanwhile, he allowed Brinna to carefully start collecting the documents to get them up off the floor. She arranged them in a careful pile, trying to determine what might be missing.

"I've only started logging these in," she said. "I'm afraid I don't have a full inventory of everything that was in the box."

"That's okay, just do your best. Is there anything missing from what you do have listed already?"

She pulled out her inventory list. Most of what she'd gone through included financial statements and interoffice memos. They were all here. She recalled finding a whole packet of expenditures, so she glanced through her pile until she determined they were present and accounted for as well. After ten minutes of study, she began to think nothing had been taken at all. Then she noticed one of the last items she'd listed on her inventory sheet.

"There was a photo…"

She searched around, moving papers and stooping to look under tables and desks. Gabe pitched in to help.

"What sort of photo?"

"It was very professional looking and matted in a cardboard frame. I'm pretty sure it was taken fifty years ago, just before the Boyston scandal."

Officer Lanford perked up when he heard that. "You mean when they were trying to build that other factory and some guy embezzled all the money?"

Brinna winced, but Gabe answered quickly. "No one ever determined who embezzled all the money. Brinna's grandfather was in charge of that project, Lanford. He has always maintained his innocence."

"He *is* innocent," Brinna declared. "He was proud of his work on that project, even if it did end badly for him. That photo was nice. He looked really good in it—so young, standing proud in his brand-new office."

"I thought they never finished that building," Lanford said. "How did he get an office?"

"They built his office first," she explained. "My grandfather and his team were supposed to lead the project from there while the attached factory was being finished. Unfortunately, once the embezzlement was discovered and the money was gone, construction had to stop. Only the frame of the factory building had been put up by then."

"Was there anyone else in the photo?" Gabe asked.

"No, just my grandpa and that big old safe everyone still tells stories about."

"You mean that safe was *real*?" Lanford said with a laugh. "I thought that was just an urban legend—an old safe abandoned out there with a million dollars still locked up in it."

"It was real," she assured him. "But of course it's not still sitting out there with money in it. After all this time and all the kids who've gone poking around out there, someone would've found it. They must've gotten rid of the safe when they cleared the office."

"Yeah, there's nothing out there now," Lanford agreed. "We all sure liked to dream about finding that money, though."

The officer was a dozen years or so older than Brinna and Gabe, but he'd obviously grown up with the same rumors and stories that they had. That old safe was legend around here. Brinna regretted the photo was suddenly missing. It meant a lot to her personally.

"You're sure that photo isn't here now?" Gabe asked.

"I don't see it anywhere. It's really a shame, because it's a valuable piece of local history."

"Maybe that's why someone took it," Lanford said.

"Maybe," she replied, but she had to admit to the rest of what she knew about it. "Or maybe it was because of the writing on the back of the photo."

"What was written on the back of it?" Gabe asked.

"Some numbers in my grandfather's handwriting," she said slowly. "I think it was the safe's combination."

Gabe wished he didn't have such a bad feeling in the pit of his stomach. Who'd broken in here? He didn't want to think about what could've happened if Brinna had been here at the time.

"So that photo is the only thing that was taken?" he asked her.

"As far as I can tell."

One of the detectives called from across the room, so Lanford left them alone to help over there. Gabe was glad to continue questioning Brinna.

"You're sure those numbers were the combination?"

"No, not at all. It was just a series of numbers, but it didn't look like a phone number or anything I recognized. I didn't think anything of them until I realized the photo was gone and we started talking about the safe. I just realized what the numbers must be."

"It sure would be a motive for someone to take the photo…as long as they also know where that safe is."

"Maybe my grandpa has some ideas about what happened to it."

"I guess that's just one more question I'll have to ask him that he won't be happy about."

"I should probably ask him about anything else that might've been in the box, too," she suggested. "I'll take it home with me tonight and finish the inventory, if that's okay with you, Officer Elliot."

"It's not okay with me," Gabe said. "Somebody broke into this place to steal from that box. Now you want to take it to your *home*? I don't think so."

"They had all afternoon to take everything in here," she argued. "I'm pretty sure they got what they wanted. I'll be safe with the box."

"Well, I don't like it. In fact, it was a mistake for me to involve you in any of this. I'm sorry, Brinna, but for your own safety, this investigation needs to be left up to the police. If you want, I'll take the box to my place and do your inventory for you. Then I'll let you know what I found, and you can ask your grandfather all about it tomorrow."

"This is property of the historical center, Gabe. I can't just send it home with you. It's my responsibility, and I'm the one who will do the inventory on it."

"Then you'll do it right here, and I'll stay with you to make sure everything is all right," he insisted.

"I'm not spending the rest of my evening here at the library. I'm going home to my cat, putting on my fuzzy socks, making a cup of tea, and sitting in my comfy chair while I work."

"Why not just hang a sign out in your front yard that says, I'm Home Alone with Valuable Secret Stuff. I'm sure our criminal would appreciate the notice."

"You're being ridiculous. It's not your place to tell me what I can and cannot do."

"It most certainly is my place. I'm the one who got you into this, Brinna, and I... I just couldn't live with myself if you got hurt."

"You didn't seem to care about hurting me ten years ago," she shot back.

They were both suddenly silent. The other investigators in the room with them went silent, too. Gabe could feel their eyes on him and wished he could erase the last minute. He shouldn't have tried to order Brinna around. She was right. It wasn't his place, and he certainly hadn't cared much about protecting her ten years ago.

"I'm sorry," he said softly after an awkward pause. "I shouldn't have told you what to do."

She looked away from him and shook her head. "No, I'm sorry. I had no right to bring up what happened ten years ago. That's all water under the bridge, and we don't need to discuss it."

"We should discuss it, Brinna," he said, his voice dropping low. "What I did to you was cruel and unfair. I can never make it up to you, and I know it's ten years overdue, but I truly apologize. I'm so sorry. You have every right to be angry with me, to call me names, even throw things at me."

For a few beats, she met his gaze with an intense look he couldn't quite decipher. Then she grabbed his arm and pulled him back into her office. Now they were alone around a lot of heavy objects. He was half afraid she would take him up on his offer and start throwing them.

But she didn't. Instead, her expression softened, and she gave him a weak smile. He was caught off guard by that more than anything else she could've done.

"Don't worry, you're safe," she said softly. "You know me, Gabe. You know what your leaving did to me, I don't need to tell you. I do need to tell you that I forgive you, though. It took some time and a lot of prayer, but I don't hold anything against you."

"Really?"

She laughed. "Really. I wasn't sure until you showed up last week. But I found out the past really is behind me. Behind both of us, I hope."

He was acutely aware of his coworkers standing just in the next room, probably eavesdropping. He was glad for that audience, in fact, or he might have done something stupid like blubber on about how much he'd missed Brinna, and how he had thought of her every day and never stopped caring about her. It was all he could do to simply return her smile and steer the conversation back to professional matters.

"You're right, it's behind us. Thank you. If you feel secure taking the papers home with you tonight, I will support that."

"Good," she said with a nod. "But just so you know, I value your opinion as a law officer, so I will take my box—and my cat—over to stay with my parents tonight. I won't be home alone, but I can wear my fuzzy socks. Is that a deal?"

"Deal," he said enthusiastically.

No doubt Gabe would get all sorts of grief from his coworkers tomorrow about his interactions with Brinna. He didn't care. If people wanted to make fun of him for groveling in front of her, let them. He'd grovel all day to hear her absolve him again.

* * *

Brinna loaded her box into Gabe's car. After she made such a big fuss about taking that box home with her, she remembered she'd walked to work today. Gabe graciously offered to drive her home so she didn't have to carry it all that way. She was tempted to turn him down just on principle, but that would've been silly.

Besides, she was feeling a little bit smug for winning their fight. He'd owed her that apology for a long time and she was glad to have finally received it. She might as well let him chauffeur her around for a bit.

"Your cat won't mind going over to your parents' house tonight?" he asked as they pulled out of the library parking lot.

"She loves it there. They have a whole setup for her—litter box, toys, a fancy climbing house. When I travel, she stays with them, and they pamper her like you cannot imagine."

"No, I can't imagine," he said, chuckling. "Wasn't your dad a stickler against pets in the house?"

She laughed at the memory. "Yes, he was. Then Ben and I grew up, and they realized the house was too empty. They got a rescue dog and call him their favorite child. He and Miss Mimi are best buds."

"I guess things *have* changed around here."

"Not everything," she assured him. "See? The sandwich shop is still there, and the bowling alley."

She pointed out a few other landmarks he would remember. He did, and he had a story for each one. They both laughed when he reminded her about the time a group of them were hanging out in town, and she found a twenty-dollar bill on the sidewalk and insisted on going into all the nearby businesses to ask if anyone had lost it. Finally, Zoey admitted *she* had dropped the money on purpose, because she wanted to go to the movies and Gabe and Brinna were broke that day, but neither of them would let Zoey pay for their ticket.

Brinna's laughter faded as she thought about her friend. "She's been a really good friend, Gabe. I'm sorry I upset her by not telling her about the investigation."

"You were trying to protect her," he said. "The same as I was. I was trying to convince myself not to take Mr. Kleinert's confession seriously. Instead…"

"Instead you found enough questions to make you start an investigation. It's not your fault, Gabe. You did the right thing, and I did the right thing. I just wish it hadn't hurt Zoey."

"Yeah, me, too. Okay, here's your house. Be on the lookout for any prowlers."

"It's still broad daylight," she noted. The days were getting longer, and sunset was still three hours away, even though it was well into the dinner hour.

"I know, I know."

He pulled into her driveway and brought the car to a stop, so she removed her seat belt and started gathering up her things. She pulled her purse over her shoulder and tucked her notebook under her arm.

"I'll get the box for you," Gabe said, jumping out and running around to her side of the car.

He probably would've opened her door for her, but she beat him to it. Instead, he opened the back door and extracted the box. She had to admit, she appreciated not having to juggle everything while she dug her keys out of her purse.

He followed her up to the door and then inside. The house was warm from the sun shining in all day. Miss Mimi peeked around the corner to greet them.

"Just put the box on the table," she said, dropping her purse and notebook there. "My grandmother had me bring home a couple of her old photo albums so I could scan some of the photos for her. I should probably take them with me. There might be other photos of my grandfather at his office."

"Oh, good thinking. I'm still not convinced the

numbers you saw on the back of that photo are the combination."

"What else could they be?" She left the kitchen and headed to the living room.

"I don't know, I didn't see them," he replied.

"Well, I did, and the combination is the only thing that makes sense," she said firmly, stooping to open the bottom drawer on the hutch in the corner. Gabe stayed in the kitchen, so she was speaking loudly now. "I'll call my grandfather tonight and ask him about it. What time do you want to meet with him tomorrow? I'll find out if he's available."

Gabe didn't reply, so she grabbed the photo albums out of the drawer and headed back to the kitchen. She found him with a packet of papers in his hands and a frown on his face.

"What is that?" she asked.

"Some of those expense reports," he said. "This one is about the construction project, payments to contractors and things like that. It looks like the last thing that was done on the building was the concrete floor. I guess they built the steel frame and then poured the concrete inside?"

She shrugged. "I guess so. That's about all that's left out there."

He was still studying the sheet. "Seems like work stopped a couple weeks before the concrete was poured. There's no record of money going out, but they still did the floor. I wonder why?"

"Who knows? Maybe it was already contracted or something."

He still wasn't content. "So was the rest of the construction. Hmm, when was the report of the embezzlement actually made, I wonder?"

"Oh, I've got that," she said, plopping the photo albums on the table with everything else. "Here, in my notebook. I've been putting together a time line. See? Construction began here, and here's where my grandfather was promoted, and here is where the embezzlement was discovered a few months later. It made headlines immediately. Payment to the construction company had gone out on Friday, and by Monday the check bounced. Mr. Boyston talked to the bank, only to discover someone had forged his name and moved all the funds from that account. They had to take money from other accounts to pay their construction bills, and for a while it was iffy whether there'd be enough to meet payroll. They filed a police report, and the expansion project stopped right then."

"Okay, so what does this mean?" Gabe poked his finger onto the time line she'd drawn. "This is when the concrete was poured."

Sure enough, his finger rested on a spot nearly two weeks after the project had been halted. *After* people were already accusing her grandfather of stealing from the company. *After* Mr. Boyston had made a public statement that the expansion project could not move forward until they got to the bottom of this discrepancy. *After* rumors of bankruptcy and insolvency began to circulate.

"But if the company was in such trouble, why would they pay for a huge concrete floor in a building they weren't going to finish?" she asked.

"Maybe I've watched too many gangster movies," Gabe began. "But missing persons and mysterious concrete flooring makes me think of just one thing."

"You don't think…there could be a body buried in that concrete out there?" She felt her mouth gape open at the very idea of it. "No, Gabe, that can't be. All this time? Surely not."

"I don't want it to be true, but it certainly would explain how someone could get murdered here in our little town, and his body never be found. It could also explain how Mr. Kleinert could've been involved in it. He was a manager with Boystons at that time."

"But so was my grandfather, and there's no way he was involved in murder. How would you even go about proving this? You can't just go out and dig up the whole factory site."

"No, I can't, and I'm pretty sure my chief won't get a court order to do that."

"So what will you do?"

"I don't know, but someone has obviously been trying to keep us from finding the truth. They're not going to be happy if that's where the body's hidden, and we've figured it out. I'm glad you're going to your parents tonight, Brinna."

When she glanced up to find him gazing at her with such earnest concern, she wondered if maybe she was standing too close. It was nearly impossible not to feel things for Gabe when he looked at her that way.

"You worry too much, Gabe," she said, trying to lighten the mood. "I don't remember you being such a worrier."

"I don't remember you ever being in danger like this."

His gaze had captured hers, and she couldn't look away. "You really think I'm in danger?"

"I don't want to take any chances. I'm staying here until you're ready to leave, then I'm following you to your parents' house."

"Gabe, that's not necessary. I'm fine."

"I'll leave if you insist, but you might as well know that I'll just park my car out front and keep an eye on you from there."

"Yeah? Well, what about you? Aren't you in danger? If someone wants to stop me from investigating, they surely will want to stop you, too."

He smiled at her. "Then I guess we both need to keep an eye on each other."

Suddenly, she realized she *was* in danger. She was falling headlong in love with this guy again, and there wasn't anything she could do about it. Maybe she'd never quite fallen out of love with him, even after everything he did. All she knew was that she could be setting herself up for heartbreak, and this time it would be so much worse because she should've known better.

She stood there, too close for comfort but frozen in place. Gabe's eyes were warm and full of all the hopes they once had shared. He reached up and touched her face, just a gentle brush with his finger. The tingle she felt was enough to unfreeze her, and she quickly stepped away.

"I've got to get my things together. You can… You can carry this stuff to my car if you want."

He graciously didn't keep staring at her. He moved away so she could pass him. "Yeah, okay. I'll do that."

ELEVEN

Gabe followed his father back into the house after their morning trip to physical therapy. He'd had a busy day already, but it was keeping his mind off Brinna. Mostly. But now it was ten thirty and he was going to meet Brinna at her grandfather's house at eleven. After that unexpected moment in her kitchen last night, his chest tightened at the thought of seeing her again.

What had he been thinking, to touch her that way? Thankfully, she'd brought him back to reality and kept her distance while she gathered her things to go to her parents. Gabe would be on his guard today and make sure to keep things purely professional.

Or maybe he should just cancel, let Brinna talk to her grandfather without him. He knew Mr. Randall wasn't going to be happy to see him, anyway. Gabe half wished his father needed his help today so he'd have an excuse not to go, but Dad was just fine. Therapy went well, and their friend Kay was on hand. She really cared about Dad and was a big part of his recovery.

Gabe was out of excuses.

"Shouldn't you be going to meet Brinna now?" his dad asked, interrupting his thoughts.

"Yes, and her grandfather."

"For your investigation. Are you sure Isaac Randall really wants to talk to you? He's never been eager to talk about what happened fifty years ago, and I doubt his attitude about it has softened now that you've dug it all up again."

Gabe could only shrug. "Brinna said he's willing."

"You've been seeing a lot of her, haven't you? Is it just for this murder business, or something else?"

"I know you told me to leave her alone, Dad. I don't need to hear it again. Yes, she's been helping me with the investigation, but—"

"But you're hoping for more?"

He didn't want to have this conversation with his father—Dad had lectured him over the phone for years. The last thing he needed today was to be reminded of how foolish and cruel he'd been to leave the way he had. How was he going to move past this if everything in his life kept reminding him of it?

"Look, Dad… I know I hurt Brinna and you and everyone in New Minden when I left like I did. It was the wrong thing to do."

162 *A Dangerous Past*

"Was it?" His father studied him, his eyes narrowed in an expression Gabe didn't quite recognize. "Was leaving here really the wrong thing to do? You mean you regret all that you've done these past ten years?"

"No, of course not," Gabe said without thinking. "I mean, not all of it. I regret some things, naturally, but that's just part of growing up."

"It is," his father agreed. "I'm glad you see that. You needed to get out of New Minden, and I guess we both understand that now. The way you went about it was wrong—that's undeniable—but leaving was right. If you're going to hold a grudge against yourself, Gabe, make sure it's for the right thing."

"Is this supposed to be some kind of pep talk?" Gabe asked, only half joking.

His father nodded. "Probably. Or a sermon. I'm pretty good at those."

"Yes, you are," Gabe agreed. "And I've got seven minutes before I need to leave, so let's hear the rest."

"Okay, here it is. I'll admit I was hurt when you took off like you did. All those years after your mother died, it was just you and me. Now you've finally come back, and I worry it's only from a grudging sense of duty. That hurts me, too. I don't want to be an invalid who needs help from his son."

"Dad, that's not how it is."

"I know, I'm starting to get it, finally. I think I understand a little."

"Understand what?"

"Why you left, why you came back, and now why this case is so important to you."

Gabe couldn't help but let out a weary sigh. "If you understand all that, I'd love to hear it."

"You do it because you *have* to," his father said simply. "You are just built to hunt for the truth, to shine light on it and bring it out in the open. That's why you had to leave, to find out who you really are. That's why you came back, too. And I'm glad you did."

"Well, thanks for that, Dad."

"But I still don't know if it's such a good idea for you to be hanging around Brinna so much. You might find some truth there you don't really like."

Gabe knew exactly what he meant. His dad might've had some struggles lately, but he was still sharp. He obviously knew Gabe wasn't quite as over Brinna as he kept saying he was. And he knew Brinna wasn't exactly still carrying a torch for his son.

"If it's truth, I'll just have to live with it, won't I? Same goes for this investigation," Gabe said. "I've got to find out what happened, what Mr. Kleinert was talking about when he gave me that confession. If it makes people angry with me, that's just how it is."

"So he really did confess to a murder?" his dad asked.

"All I can say is Chief Seigle felt there was reason to open an investigation."

"I just wish… Well, I was Dwight Kleinert's pastor all this time. He should have opened up to me about it, for his sake. He did a lot of good things for the church, but… I always suspected there were some shadows in his past."

"What made you think that?"

"Well, he was…burdened. He volunteered for just about every project here, but he never seemed satisfied with his efforts, never let me thank him for his hard work. He always brushed it off. I got the feeling he was trying to prove something to himself and always ended up disappointed."

"As if he had a guilty conscience?"

"I don't know about that, but there's also that invisible brick wall between Brinna's family and his. As long as I've been here, it's common knowledge that there's no love lost between the two families. I was always surprised the families allowed Brinna and Zoey to become such good friends. And now Zoey's marrying Ben."

"Were the families really so hostile toward each other?"

"Years ago, Dwight was a faithful attendee at the same church with Isaac, Brinna's grandfather. They were friends as boys, even. About the time of the Boyston scandal, though, the whole Kleinert family left that church and moved their membership here. That was long before I served here, of course, but I heard all about it. Maybe when you talk to Isaac, he can tell you why…if he'll talk about it at all."

"I hope he will. So, is the sermon done? I've got to head out."

His father smiled and waved his hands dismissively. "Go, go. Kay is fixing me some lunch, so I won't miss you at all. Go do your cop things."

"All right, Dad. I'm glad you're in good hands."

"And you say hi to Brinna for me."

"I will."

Gabe was still smiling when he headed back out to his car. Things weren't always relaxed between him and his dad, but he appreciated knowing his father understood what he was doing. That made all the side glances and headshaking he'd been given at church just a little easier to take. He had somehow earned his father's respect, and that was a great feeling.

Now he was off to see Brinna and hopefully earn a bit more of hers.

"Here you go, Grandpa," Brinna said, bringing a cup of tea to her grandfather.

He sat in his favorite chair, and sunlight streamed through the bay window in the spacious family room of his home. Her mother was raised in this house, and by all accounts, it had changed little in all the years since. There was a formal living room at the front of the house, but Brinna hardly remembered being in there. Christmases, birthday parties, and most of their family gatherings had been here in this bright space.

Brinna had heard whispers that during the difficult times after the big scandal, the family nearly lost the house because they couldn't make payments. Somehow, though, her grandparents had gotten them through. If her grandfather had embezzled that money, he certainly hadn't used it. The house showed its age.

"What time did you say that boy will be here?" Grandpa asked, poking at his cell phone and grumbling in frustration.

"Anytime now," she replied. "What's the matter? Having trouble with your phone again?"

"No, I just can't get into this account I've got."

"Forget your password?"

"I never forget my passwords. I've got a system for that, my own special code. What I don't have are tiny little fingers for pressing all these miniature buttons."

"Here, let me help you."

She was glad he wasn't afraid of modern technology, but it was nice that she was able to help him. Sure enough, he recited his password, and she typed it in. The application opened immediately.

"See? My code works perfectly. I've used it for years. I write my passwords somewhere handy, but I use my code. For all the odd numbers, I substitute a digit two numbers higher—"

"And for all the evens, it's two numbers lower, right?"

"That's right. You pay attention—you've got some good sense, even if I'm not too sure about you bringing Gabe around here."

"Thanks for meeting with him, even though I know you'd probably rather not."

Grandpa chuckled and sipped his hot tea. "You're right about that. But I don't see a way to avoid it. People are all talking about this investigation, which means they're right back to talking about me. I might as well tell Gabe what I know, which is nothing, by the way."

"I know, I know. You don't have to convince me, Grandpa. I know you wouldn't have anything to do with embezzlement, or murder."

"Well, I guess I'll just have to convince your old boyfriend, too."

"You're not going to be, um, angry with him, are you?"

"About what? Suspecting me of murder, or leaving you at the altar ten years ago?"

"Any of it. Gabe's not a bad guy, and he's

changed a lot since we knew him. He just wants to hear your side of the story, to ask you some questions about the people you knew back then. I promise, he doesn't think you're guilty of anything."

"I guess we'll find out about that, won't we?"

Right on time, the doorbell rang at the front of the house.

"I guess we will," Brinna said, taking a deep breath to calm her nerves. "You don't have to be best friends with him, Grandpa, but please give him the benefit of the doubt, okay?"

"I won't bite the man, Brinna. Go get the door, and we'll see what he wants to ask me."

She trusted her grandfather—she did—but she couldn't help feeling anxious. He'd been very frank about his feelings toward Gabe when they got word he'd come back to town, and it was unlikely that he'd softened in the past few weeks. Brinna's whole family wasn't thrilled that she and Gabe had struck up a friendship again, and they certainly weren't happy she was helping him with this investigation. For Brinna's family, Gabe Elliot and the Boyston scandal were the two topics they diligently avoided. Today, Grandpa was being asked to face both.

Brinna made her way through the house to the front door. As expected, Gabe was waiting on the front porch. She could read the nervousness all over his face—it mirrored the butterflies in her own stomach.

"Come on in," she offered, swinging the door wide for him.

He paused and peered over her shoulder as if a pet gorilla might be about to pounce on him. "Hi, Brinna. Is your grandfather sure this is a good time for me to meet with him?"

"He's fine with it. Come on, keeping him waiting isn't going to win any brownie points."

"I'm pretty sure just showing up today isn't going to, either," Gabe muttered, following her inside.

She was glad he'd come, even if it didn't seem that he was. It was a shame he was so nervous about talking to her grandfather, though. They used to be pretty good friends. Gabe didn't have grandparents of his own, so he'd sort of adopted Brinna's, and they'd certainly taken him under their wing. It was quite a blow when things ended the way they did.

She led him back to the family room, where Grandpa waited. Gabe cleared his throat and smiled almost sheepishly. For a moment, he looked just like the boy she had known all those years ago. Then the moment passed, and he collected himself, standing tall and reaching to shake Grandpa's hand.

"It's good to see you again, Mr. Randall."

Grandpa narrowed his eyes as he studied Gabe. Brinna held her breath for half a second, then Grandpa stood up and took Gabe's outstretched hand. It was quite a relief. They'd survived the most awkward part of the reunion. Now maybe they could all relax a little bit and get down to business.

"So you're here to ask me about my time working for Boyston Industries," Grandpa said.

Gabe nodded. "Yes, and I know that's not your favorite subject. I'm just hoping maybe something you remember from that time might help me put the pieces together on this murder investigation."

Grandpa offered Gabe the chair across from him, and the two of them sat. Brinna had already brought a pitcher of iced tea and some glasses into the room, so she calmed her nerves by pouring a glass for each of them. Gabe accepted his eagerly, but Grandpa was a bit more subdued.

"So Dwight Kleinert confessed to covering up a murder, but he didn't tell you who did it." Grandpa sipped his tea and got right to the heart of the matter. "I never had any inkling about it myself, but I can't say I'm shocked. There was some shady stuff going on back then. We just never figured out exactly what."

Gabe quickly put down his tea and pulled out

a notebook. "When you say 'we,' who are you primarily referring to?"

"The top management staff," Grandpa clarified. "That would be Clement and Carolyn, Dwight, and—"

"You mean Clement and Carolyn Boyston, along with Dwight Kleinert?"

"Yes. Clement didn't like to share authority, so he kept a pretty tight hand on things back then. Carolyn was his vice president, and Dwight was the production manager. We just had the one factory then, so he pretty much ran that place. I was one of the foremen there, until I got promoted up to project manager on the new facility."

"I'm told Mr. Kleinert wasn't too happy about that," Gabe noted.

Grandpa had a hearty laugh. "No, he was not. He felt like he should've been given that position, although I never understood why. As production manager, he got paid way more than I did, and he had that nice fancy office in the executive building. The new plant manager at the old site had to answer to him, and so did I over at the new plant we were building."

"Maybe he was the one doing the embezzling and was afraid you'd find out about it," Brinna suggested.

Grandpa merely shrugged. "I don't know. They never found any evidence of it, and I'm certainly not going to cast blame on someone just because he wasn't very friendly to me."

"So who else was in a position to access those accounts?" Gabe asked. "We've made a list of names we found in reports from the time, but I'm hoping you might have someone to add."

"Who's on your list?" Grandpa asked.

Brinna quickly pulled the crumpled sheet of paper out of her pocket and read aloud.

"Shirley Boyston-Jones; her husband, Renner Jones; Tammy Crenshaw, the secretary; Bob Afton, the young foreman; and an outside investor, Barty Swenson."

"Shirley was awfully young back then," the older man said thoughtfully. "I don't think she or Renner were very involved in the business. It's probably a good idea for you to talk to them, but I doubt they'll have anything new to add. Tammy will talk your ear off, but she won't know more than she's told everyone in town over the years. And Bob Afton? Yeah, he'd be one to talk to... except that he's in memory care over at the Willow Dell nursing home. Doesn't know his own family anymore, I hear."

"Oh, that's sad," Brinna said, sending Gabe a disappointed glance. "We were hoping he might have something to add. He worked directly with you on the new facility, right?"

"They assigned him to me, yes. I never quite

knew why, because he didn't strike me as very qualified. I told Dwight I should've been a part of the hiring process, since Bob would be my foreman once the new factory was up and running, but Dwight didn't much care about my opinions on things then."

"What was Bob's job description?" Gabe asked.

"Well, he was basically just doing errands for me, running paperwork back and forth to the corporate offices, things like that. We didn't have a factory to run yet, so there really wasn't any work for him to do. Sometimes I felt like he was put there to keep an eye on me."

"You thought Dwight had him spying on you?" Brinna said.

The older man shrugged. "Maybe. Like I said, he wasn't happy about me getting that promotion. When my gun went missing, I thought for sure either Dwight or Bob had taken it."

"Gun?" Gabe said. "You had a gun that went missing? When was it taken?"

"Oh, I guess I noticed it missing a couple weeks before everything fell apart. I kept it in my desk at the jobsite."

"Why did you keep a gun, Grandpa?" Brinna asked.

"All the payroll money was going to be kept in my safe. I figured I might need a little protection. One day, it just wasn't there. I never found out who took it; the lock was broken and it was just gone. There were so many people through there every day. Clement loved to bring his cronies around to show off the progress. Anyone could've taken it."

"Did it ever turn up?" Brinna asked.

"Nope. I reported it to the police chief, but he never found anything. Then I got so caught up in the embezzlement scandal that I forgot about it. Someone probably just sold it, not that they'd get much for a little snubnose .38 revolver like that."

Gabe was obviously very intrigued by this new revelation. A juicy scandal, a possible murder, *and* a missing gun? Brinna knew it had to be connected. Too bad Bob Afton wasn't able to tell them his side of the story. Did Dwight really hire him to spy on Grandpa? That would mean someone suspected him of questionable activities. Or maybe it meant someone was trying to keep him from learning of their questionable activities.

"Is there anyone else who might have information?" Gabe questioned. "Anyone we haven't thought of?"

Grandpa chewed his lip for a moment before replying. "Well, there was Gary Laughton, the comptroller. I always thought he had the easiest access to that account, but they ruled him out pretty quickly. He was out of town on some kind of family vacation when the money went missing."

"Is he still around? I'd love to ask him a few questions." Gabe said.

Grandpa shook his head. "Sorry, he was in his fifties at the time, so he's long gone now. I can't think of anyone else who… Wait, what was that last name on your list?"

Brinna glanced at her list and then replied in unison with Gabe.

"Barty Swenson."

"How'd you find out about him?" Grandpa asked. "I haven't thought about him in years and years."

"I found his name listed in an old article from before the scandal," Brinna explained. "It talked about how he was an investor from out of town. Did you know him?"

"I did," Grandpa confirmed. "At least, as well as any of us knew him. That con artist weaseled his way into Clement's pocket and told a fine story about having a million dollars to invest."

"He didn't have a million dollars?" Gabe asked.

"If he did, I never saw it. He sure had Clement convinced, though. I always thought that was why it was so easy for the embezzler—whoever it was—to steal the money. Clement thought he had access to all kinds of cash whenever he might need it, so he let his guard down. Someone drew up the paperwork, forged Clement's name, and sent it off to the bank and poof, the money was gone. By the time anyone noticed it missing, it had been transferred so many times that it was impossible to track. It ended up offshore somewhere. When Clement panicked and started pulling funds from other accounts to pay bills, he suddenly realized he couldn't access nearly as much as he thought he could."

"Where was Barty Swenson by that time?" Brinna asked.

"Oh, he hung around for a while. He got Clement to pay off his hotel bills and things like that, while he kept promising his money was being transferred and was held up on some little delay somewhere. Once he drained all he could out of Clement, he just ran off. I heard he had some girl, and they simply hopped on a train and took off. If he ever did have a million dollars, he must've taken it with him."

"That checks out with what we found about him," Brinna mused. "He had a wife and son in New Jersey, but he never went back home to them. Did you ever hear anything about who this girlfriend of his was?"

"No. People all talked about it," Grandpa said, "but nobody really knew. Some thought Swenson had been fooling around with Tammy Crenshaw, but she denied it, and she certainly didn't leave town with him."

"So there wasn't a missing woman when Swenson left?" Gabe asked, furiously making notes as they spoke.

"None that I knew about, but you've got to remember, I was thrown into the thick of things at that time, getting raked over the coals with everyone thinking I stole that money and nearly bankrupted the town." Grandpa scowled at the memories. "If there had been talk of who that woman was, I might've missed it."

"But Tammy might know more about that," Brinna said. "If people thought she was involved with Swenson, maybe she knows who actually was."

"She might," Grandpa acknowledged. "She made it a point to know what everyone was doing back then. She liked having all the secrets, but then she'd blab them all. No secret was safe around Tammy. That's why I'm pretty sure that if she knew anything about the embezzlement, she wouldn't have kept quiet all this time. Same thing for the murder. She would've told someone. I remember how furious Mr. Boyston was when Tammy let the cat out of the bag about Shirley and Renner getting married. Clement was planning on some big announcement, but Tammy went around telling people."

"Wait… Shirley Boyston and Renner Jones getting married was a secret?" Brinna asked. "Why?"

"Oh, it was right in the heat of the scandal," Grandpa replied. "I guess with everything going on and all of the Boyston financial troubles, Shirley and Renner took off and got married rather than making a big fuss with an engagement and a fancy wedding."

"So in the middle of that giant scandal, they just went and got married? That seems like unusual timing," Gabe said.

"It surprised all of us," Grandpa admitted. "From what I recall, Shirley was still in college and enjoying life. She didn't act like a girl who wanted to settle down. We all thought she seemed a little…wild at the time. Some thought she might be afraid her rich father was about to be broke, so she said yes to a nice conservative young man with well-to-do parents."

"They weren't even engaged?" Brinna questioned.

"Not that I knew, but of course, I didn't run around with the Boystons. News of their marriage came out of the blue, and Clement didn't like what that seemed to imply. I was too busy trying to stay out of jail to pay attention to any of the details. Was it a shotgun wedding? Did she marry for the money? Who knows? I'm sure

Shirley and Renner will only give the answer they want to give about that topic. Like I said, you might find out more about it from Tammy."

Gabe was still taking notes. Grandpa had given them more information than she'd expected. When Gabe looked up from his notebook, Brinna knew he felt the same. Grandpa had set aside his personal feelings, and this meeting had gone better than either of them had expected.

Now Brinna had to figure out how to convince Gabe to let her go along with him to talk to Tammy Crenshaw. It seemed they were tantalizingly close to finding more clues, maybe even untangling this whole mystery.

"Tammy's been coming to our monthly cookbook club for years," she mentioned, hoping Gabe would take the hint. "She might be more comfortable talking to someone she knows."

Grandpa clucked his tongue and gave her a dramatic eye roll. "You know perfectly well that Tammy Crenshaw doesn't need to feel comfortable to talk anyone's ears off."

Brinna scowled at him, but Gabe simply chuckled.

"Then I'll definitely need someone to tag along with me," he said, grinning at Brinna. "Sounds like extra ears will come in handy."

TWELVE

Gabe turned the air-conditioning up in his car. It was still early June, but summer was in full swing today. Brinna said goodbye to her grandfather while he called Tammy Crenshaw to set up a meeting with her. He had just ended the call when Brinna appeared, waving behind her as she shut her grandparents' front door.

"Did you get hold of her?" she asked as she hopped into the passenger seat.

"I did, actually," he replied. "Dispatch got me her number, and she answered right away. She seems like quite a character—knew my name and was eager to talk to me. In fact…she wants us to come meet her right now."

"Right now? I thought maybe we'd go get some lunch first. I'm starved."

"We'll actually be multitasking. She wants us to meet her at The Pie & Piper. She's having lunch there with a friend of hers."

"Well, that's convenient. She won't mind us

interrupting her lunch? What about her friend? Is it ethical to discuss the investigation with an audience?"

"When the audience is Shirley Boyston-Jones, I think it's a safe bet."

Brinna looked shocked. "She's having lunch with Shirley? Right at this very moment?"

"Yeah, and they'd love to have us join them. Are you up for that?"

"Absolutely. We'll cover two interviews at one time and still fit in some pie for dessert. What could be better?"

"I called my chief this morning while Dad was in physical therapy. We discussed our suspicions regarding the strange timing of the concrete they poured at the jobsite."

"You mean the concrete they poured two weeks *after* they shut down the whole project? With no official payment showing up in the books? Did he think it was as suspicious as we do?"

"I didn't expect him to, but…"

"But?"

"But he listened to me. Of course, he told me that digging up the whole site is out of the question, but when I mentioned bringing in a GPR unit, he didn't flat out say no."

She wrinkled her brow. "What's a GPR unit?"

"Ground penetrating radar," he explained. "We don't have to dig the place up. With the GPR, a team can just scan the surface and get readings of anything unusual below. If anomalies show up, we pursue a warrant to dig."

"Don't tell me you happen to have one of these GPR things just lying around."

"No, but the state investigative team does. The chief called them this morning. He just texted to say they've got us on the schedule for tomorrow afternoon. It's not public information yet, so don't go around mentioning it, but I thought you deserved to know."

"Thanks. I'm just amazed that things are moving forward so quickly. My grandpa welcomed you with open arms, we've got this instant interview with two of the top witnesses on our list, and your chief's calling in the big guys to start hunting for a body. Things are suddenly falling into place. Is it just me, or does this all seem surprisingly easy?"

"Too easy, if you ask me. We still don't have evidence to prove anything, and we might not find any. These ladies might have no information for us, and the radar might only see dirt. We haven't really accomplished anything yet."

"Yes, we have," she insisted. "*You* have. More than anything, you gave Mr. Kleinert peace in his last days, and maybe this time something good will come of everyone talking about this. If nothing else, maybe you'll get a nice big promotion.

Clearly, your chief is impressed with you, or he wouldn't have put that call in this morning."

"Okay, I am a little bit excited about that. Chief Seigle said the information we've gathered so far is convincing and impossible to ignore. It's clear that something happened here fifty years ago, and he wants to know what it was."

"That's wonderful, Gabe. And I've got to say, lining up an interview with the Boystons' private secretary *and* the current CEO herself is kind of a big deal. You're on a roll today."

"I couldn't have figured out half of this without your help, Brinna. We've been a good team. Thanks for trusting me enough to work with me."

"You lured me in with history," she said, laughing lightly.

"We've certainly got history," he said nearly under his breath.

She heard him, though. He focused on backing the car out of the driveway, but he could see her smiling from the corner of his eye. He liked it when she smiled.

"Yes, we do. Now, let's go to lunch."

Gabe wasn't in uniform today, but he still felt all eyes on him as they walked into the restaurant. Or maybe all eyes were on Brinna. She always had such a brightness to her that people couldn't help but notice her. At least Gabe had always noticed her, and that certainly hadn't changed.

He told the hostess they were meeting Ms. Crenshaw and Mrs. Boyston-Jones. She seemed to have been expecting them. Gabe recognized Shirley right away as the hostess led them toward a table at the back of the dining area. The woman with Shirley must be Ms. Crenshaw. She saw them approaching and began waving as if they were old friends. Shirley, as expected, was much more subdued.

"Good afternoon, ladies," Gabe said as they stepped up to the table. "Thank you so much for inviting us to join you here. I'm Gabe Elliot, and I'm sure you know Brinna Jenson. She works with the library and runs the history center."

"Oh yes, we know Brinna," Ms. Crenshaw said with a broad smile. "She and I go to church together. And of course you worked with her, Shirley, when they were first building the history center for your mother."

Shirley gave a gracious nod and motioned toward the two empty chairs at their table. "Yes, Brinna was a great favorite of my mother's. Won't you both sit down? I have to say, I was more than a little surprised when Tammy said you phoned her this morning, Mr. Elliot. Or should I call you Officer Elliot? Or Reverend? It seems you have quite a few titles, young man."

"Gabe is just fine," he assured her, not quite certain if she was being flattering, or if there was something just a bit condescending in her tone.

The ladies tittered, and he slid a questioning glance toward Brinna. She gave him the hint of a shrug and politely took the seat that was offered to her. Gabe had no idea if they were about to learn anything useful, but this was bound to be an interesting lunch, that much was certain.

The waiter came around to bring their beverages and take their orders. The menu was a little more upscale than what he was used to, but Brinna seemed to feel right at home. She ordered a soup and salad, so he did the same. Tammy quickly got all the necessary small talk out of the way. They determined that both ladies were well acquainted with Gabe's and Brinna's families. Tammy seemed to know all about Gabe's military service as well as Brinna's world travels and her volunteer work with local high school students. Shirley practically beamed with pride when Brinna's brother was mentioned.

"Oh, we couldn't get by without Ben at Boyston Industries," Shirley said. "I don't know what we'll do when he goes off on his honeymoon for two full weeks."

"Zoey laid down the law on that one." Brinna chuckled. "I think if it were up to Ben, he'd go right back to work the day after the wedding."

Shirley nodded. "He's such a big part of our Boytson family. And Zoey now, too, of course."

"And isn't that what you both came to talk to us about today?" Tammy said brightly. "We're all dying to know what you've found out in this investigation of yours, Gabe. A murder, right here in New Minden. Who would've ever thought?"

"We don't know there *was* a murder," Shirley corrected, then she turned to Gabe for confirmation. "Isn't that right?"

"Yes, it is. I was given a confession by an elderly patient—"

"Dwight Kleinert was as straight as an arrow," Tammy chirped. "I can't believe he'd ever be mixed up in murder."

"Neither can I," Shirley agreed. "But apparently, you believed him, Gabe? Even though he was heavily medicated and not entirely in his right mind at the time."

Before Gabe could answer, Brinna chimed in. "It's not up to Gabe to believe people or not. He's a police officer. It's his responsibility to serve and protect. If someone tells him a crime was committed, he's duty bound to take it seriously and find out about it."

"That's all we're trying to do," he added. "Since the possible crime happened so long ago, I asked Brinna with her expertise in research and access to the historical archives to help me dig into things."

"And what have you found?" Shirley asked.

Gabe carefully deflected her question. "We've been studying old news reports and police records regarding the financial scandal that rocked Boyston Industries fifty years ago. Since the two of you were at least present then—I know you were both very young at the time—I'd love for you to answer a few questions about what you remember."

He hoped that mentioning their age back then wasn't too much obvious flattery, but neither of them seemed to take offense. Tammy, in fact, grinned at him.

"Oh, I'm older than I look, young man. Shirley is a spring chicken next to me. She was still in college back then, but I was working for Mr. Boyston himself. I remember a lot of what went on back in those days. It was such a difficult time. Go ahead, ask your questions."

"All right. Thank you, Ms. Crenshaw. I'll try not to waste anyone's time by going over things that have been public knowledge for decades now. I guess I'll just start with the big question. Did you have any idea, any suspicion, that someone had been murdered?" Gabe asked.

Shirley dropped her salad fork and made a slight choking sound. "Well, that certainly cuts right to the chase. Honestly, Mr. Elliot, how can you ask something like that? If any of us had thought such a thing back then, don't you think we would've reported it?"

"I'm not suggesting you *knew* anything happened, I'm just asking if there was ever a moment when you *wondered*. Maybe it seemed far-fetched back then, but now that this has come up, maybe you realize it was plausible?"

Tammy answered before Shirley could. "I'm sure all sorts of things ran through our minds back then. I know I certainly wondered about some things."

"What sort of things?" Gabe asked her.

"How someone got that money, of course. It was done so efficiently. They had all the right paperwork and everything was in order. The police showed it to me, and honestly, if I didn't know better, I would've sworn Mr. Boyston himself got that money from the bank."

"But he didn't," Shirley interjected. "Someone else put all the paperwork together and transferred that money out of the account. And there was never any talk about a murder back then. No one was missing, so how could we suspect murder?"

"Well, there was Barty," Tammy added. "He went missing."

Shirley shot her a heated glance. "That con man had nothing to do with anything."

Tammy shrugged. "Of course, we don't talk about Barty Swenson."

"Well, I'd like to hear about Barty Swenson," Gabe said. "He doesn't show up in the police reports or newspapers. Why was everyone so certain he had nothing to do with the embezzlement?"

"He only left town *after* the money was stolen," Shirley replied. "Once he realized my father didn't have anything left to give him. He was just a con artist, dangling my father along with promises he never intended to keep."

The server brought their food, but it sat there neglected. It was surprising to hear so much emotion in Shirley's voice. Gabe hadn't expected that. From what little he knew of her, Shirley Boyston was cool and professional. He was taken aback to see her react with this much passion even after all this time.

"Where did Barty Swenson go?" Brinna asked, jumping into the conversation.

"He left town by train," Shirley replied. "With a woman."

"Who was the woman?" Gabe asked.

"No one knows," Tammy said, dropping her voice as if this was suddenly a big secret. "That was quite the mystery back then. People had seen him around town with a woman, but no one could ever say who it was. When he left like that…

Oh, you should have heard the gossip. Can you believe that some people even said he'd run off with me. How on earth would such a rumor like that even get started?"

"You weren't involved with Mr. Swenson?" Gabe asked.

"Certainly not. That man had a wife and child out east somewhere. I wouldn't run around with a married man, though he did try to catch my eye. He flirted with all the girls. Remember how he used to flip your ponytail, Shirley? He called you Twirly as I recall."

"No, I don't remember that. I barely remember him at all," Shirley said. "I was dating Renner back then, so I didn't pay attention to Barty."

"Well, other girls around town did," Tammy noted. "I'm pretty sure he had something going with one of them. He'd come back to the office after a long lunch hour, and he'd smell like an aftershave commercial. We all figured he was meeting someone on the sly. He seemed the type."

"Someone here in New Minden?" Brinna asked.

"I think so," Tammy replied. "But no one ever admitted to it after he was gone. Whoever she was, I can't say I blame her. I'd not want to be known as *that* kind of girl."

"Whoever he was meeting was local, someone he could see on a lunch hour," Brinna said. "But if he left with a woman from town, why didn't anyone know who she was?"

Gabe agreed. "People would've noticed that she was gone. Did any local women leave town during that time?"

Both older ladies looked at each other and then shrugged.

"No," Shirley said. "That's why it's a mystery. If Barty did have a girl here in town, she didn't leave with him."

"But Howard at the train station saw them," Tammy pointed out. "Remember? He showed the police his ticket book. There were two tickets sold to Barty Swenson that night, and he was traveling with a lady."

Gabe had his notebook out now. "Did that ticket book give her name?"

Brinna was ready with the answer for that. "No, they only recorded the name of the purchaser and no one had to show ID."

"So she could have been anyone," Gabe said, frustrated. "How many days was this after the embezzlement came to light?"

"Gosh, I don't know," Tammy said. "It seems like it all happened at once, but who can remember?"

"It was a long time ago," Shirley agreed. "I wasn't even here. I was at college. I came home after the theft came to light because my father wanted me nearby. But all of this must be in the police reports, Gabe. If you want specific dates and times, you'll need to check them."

"Yes, I'll do that," Gabe assured her. He'd already read through everything on the subject, but it couldn't hurt to go over it all again. "So that's everything you remember about Barty Swenson?"

"Yep," Shirley replied. "I'm sorry we can't help you identify your murdered person. Maybe it's all just a misunderstanding, anyway. I'm sure Mr. Kleinert didn't intentionally mislead you about this, but he was awfully sick. You haven't found a body yet, have you?"

"No. We haven't," Gabe confirmed.

Shirley shook her head in concern. "I hope there isn't a body to find. It would be awful to think someone's been missing all this time, and no one ever knew it."

"Someone knew it," Gabe assured her. "And Barty Swenson *has* been missing all this time. His wife and his son never saw him again."

THIRTEEN

Brinna tried to digest all the information they were getting from Shirley and Tammy at their lunch table. She wasn't sure what to make of it. Was Gabe hearing anything that she wasn't? He certainly was taking plenty of notes.

So far, the ladies had confirmed the things Brinna and Gabe had already learned from other sources. The company couldn't meet payroll one week, which caused a panic and the building site shut down. There was an immediate audit of the books, which led to the discovery of embezzlement. That part was confusing. She couldn't figure out how the auditors were able to confirm that Barty Swenson wasn't the culprit, yet they couldn't find out who was?

Brinna was just about to ask Shirley for clarification when Tammy interrupted the conversation with a squeal of delight.

"Oh, look. It's Mr. Snare. Over here, Mr. Snare. Come join us."

Tammy waved enthusiastically at Pete Snare. He'd just come into the restaurant and was being led to a table on the other side of the room, but he smiled and waved back at Tammy. His face brightened when he noticed her companions.

Brinna was pretty sure she caught Gabe rolling his eyes as Pete started coming their way.

"Ms. Crenshaw, how lovely to see you again," Pete said when he reached their table. "And Brinna, what a surprise to find you here, too. I guess it's true what they say about a small town—everyone really does know everyone else."

"Hello, Pete," Brinna said. "I guess you've met Tammy, and this is Gabe Elliot."

Pete held out his hand to Gabe. "Oh, right, I've heard about you. The minister cop, right? I'm Pete Snare, writer."

Gabe politely gave the man a handshake, but it didn't look like a hearty one. "Yes, Brinna mentioned you were in town doing some research. How's that been going for you? Have you found what you were looking for?"

Pete didn't appear to notice the slight accusatory tone behind Gabe's questions. He simply smiled and turned his attentions to Shirley.

"Yes, I think I have, as a matter of fact. And let me guess…you must be Shirley Boyston-Jones."

Shirley looked surprised that he knew her name. "Er, yes. So you're in town doing research?"

Tammy jumped in to provide an explanation, except that her account of Mr. Snare's work only added to Brinna's confusion of this whole bizarre meetup.

"Pete is writing a book about rural women of past decades who chose to leave the farm and enter the corporate world," Tammy said. "I let him interview me a couple days ago. He wanted to know all about how I grew up here in Minden County, went off to secretary school, and then had a wonderful career with Boyston Industries."

Pete looked embarrassed when he glanced at Brinna. "I've been finding a lot of great material here in New Minden on a couple different topics. I'll probably get two or three books out of it, in fact."

"I'll look forward to reading them," Brinna said, doubtful she'd ever have that opportunity.

What was Pete Snare up to? She hadn't thought much about it when he said he was researching railroads, but why would he give a completely different story to Tammy? Now that she thought about it, he hadn't asked a lot of questions about the railroad, and his research seemed to have been rather limited. Apparently, though, it wasn't very limited at all. It sounded as if he'd been asking Tammy all sorts of questions about her time working for the Boystons.

Gabe had already been somewhat suspicious

of the man, and now he was eyeing him with an icy stare. Pete was too busy being fawned over by Tammy to notice. She insisted that the hostess pull up a chair and let Pete join their table. Shirley didn't seem too happy with this new addition, but she made some space and let Tammy happily chatter about how nice it was to run into Pete this way.

"So, Pete, how long are you sticking around for this?" Gabe asked once Pete was settled in and had ordered a hamburger platter.

"Oh, I think a few more days. I'm not sure," Pete replied, turning to Shirley. "I was actually going to give you a call, Ms. Boyston-Jones, to see if you would sit down with me to answer a few more questions about your family's business. Tammy had so much to say about it that I'm wondering if I could possibly do a whole book about the history of your family here in New Minden."

"Well… I suppose we could schedule something. I've been awfully busy, though. We've got a lot going on right now." Shirley was sweet, but Brinna could tell she was not excited about setting up an interview.

Tammy—in her usual way—inserted herself into the discussion with information nobody asked for. "Oh, things have been very busy at Boyston's corporate offices, that's for sure. I'm glad I'm retired, or I'm sure I'd be run ragged.

Shirley's right-hand man is getting married in about ten days, and he'll be gone for a nice long honeymoon, so they're all racing around to get things caught up before he leaves. And on top of it all, there's a big party for him on Friday night. Oh, all the staff will be there, and even some retired folks like me. It's going to be really fun."

"Wow, the company is putting on a big party for this guy getting married?" Pete asked. "That sounds like a good time. And it's for everyone on staff to attend?"

"All the corporate and management staff," Shirley answered. "We're like a family at Boyston Industries. Ben and Zoey are a big part of our team, and we're all very happy to celebrate their upcoming day."

"Ben is Brinna's brother," Tammy added. "You'll be at the party on Friday, won't you, Brinna?"

"Yes, I'm planning to be there," Brinna answered, wondering how they'd gotten onto this subject.

"Gabe will probably be there, too," Tammy said quickly. "He's the minister doing the wedding. Aren't you, Gabe?"

"Yes, I am," Gabe confirmed. "But I'm not sure what my schedule will be on Friday."

"Oh, you have to come," Tammy said. "You

can come with Brinna. It's so good to see you two together again."

Brinna opened her mouth quickly to correct Tammy's mistake. "No, we're not—"

But Tammy was already off on another tangent. "I'm so excited to see how the new conference center at the Boyston headquarters will be decorated. Now you can host big events in the very same building where you work, Shirley. Boy, that would've been handy back in my day. When your father put on a big dinner or something, I had to make do with whatever rental space was available."

"Yes, I think this will be a nice feature for us," Shirley agreed. "This building project and all the renovations were a lot of work, but it was needed after Boyston Industries' growth."

"How many facilities do you have now?" Pete asked.

Brinna was thrilled that the conversation had moved on to less personal topics. Shirley clearly enjoyed talking about her work, and she told Pete all about the main manufacturing facility, the newly expanded corporate headquarters, and the state-of-the-art warehouse and processing building that had been put in five or six years ago.

Brinna gave Gabe a relieved smile and was able to finish her salad. Gabe returned her smile, but his expression toward Pete didn't warm. He clearly didn't like the guy. Maybe it was because Pete asked so many questions about things that didn't really fit with what he claimed he was working on. Or maybe it was because he'd taken up so much of Brinna's time with his so-called research. She kind of hoped that might be part of Gabe's reasoning. It would be nice to think he'd rather have her spend the time with *him* instead of a dubious stranger off the street.

"Boyston Industries has been the lifeblood of New Minden for generations," Tammy said. "Everyone has some connection to it, and it's a part of the folklore of our town."

"So I've been hearing," Pete said. "I met a few young people on my first day in town who told me about an old abandoned factory site out in the countryside. They seemed to think it might even be haunted."

Brinna caught Gabe's eye. He seemed as intrigued by this as she was. Just who hadn't Pete talked to in his short stay in New Minden?

Shirley didn't look impressed by Pete's knowledge of local ghost stories. "That's ridiculous. Of course that old site isn't haunted. It's just a derelict worksite where my father tried to build another factory. When the company hit some financial difficulties, the project was scrapped before it barely got off the ground. There's nothing out there."

But Pete wasn't giving up so easily. "One of the kids told me a story about an old safe with a million dollars in it…"

"Oh, that old fable." Shirley rolled her eyes and laughed. "No truth to it, of course. Does anyone really think my father would've left a million dollars lying around like that? What rubbish. Anything of value was quickly moved back to our offices when the project was scrapped."

"So there *was* a safe with a million dollars in it?" Pete asked.

Shirley gave him an even glare. "Well, I never found a million dollars sitting around. People just like to talk."

"Yes, they certainly do," Pete agreed. "I've talked to a lot of people since I've been here. Who would've thought this little town could have so many interesting stories? A lot of them seem to go back to the same time period about fifty years ago. That's about the same time of the murder you're investigating, isn't it?" Pete said and turned to Gabe.

Brinna didn't like the cold gleam in Pete's eye. For the first time, she understood what he was really researching. He was after information about the same thing they were, but how had he even learned about it? He'd started his research before Gabe started the official investigation. What did Pete know that they didn't?

"I can't talk about an ongoing investigation," Gabe said firmly. "Unless you have information that you think would be helpful to the police?"

"Seems like the police have had plenty of time to figure things out," Pete said. "Fifty years is a long time to ignore a missing person, isn't it? But you're on it now. I'm sure you don't need any help from me."

Brinna was surprised Pete had said something so harsh. She could see Gabe was quietly fuming, but Pete merely chewed his lunch with a smug look on his face. Brinna wondered why he would want to insult the police this way. Shirley must be wondering the same thing. She went very silent and pushed a cucumber slice around her plate. Tammy, however, missed all the subtext and rambled on with her customary enthusiasm.

"I just think New Minden must be the nicest little town in Ohio. What do you think, Pete? You've been going around doing your research. How does New Minden stack up with some of the other towns you've visited?"

"Oh, it's the most memorable, for sure," Pete answered with a hint of laughter. "I would say New Minden has plenty of hidden treasures."

Tammy agreed, telling him about some of the things she loved best about New Minden. It didn't completely ease the tension between everyone, but it was nice to hear so many positive things.

Brinna encouraged the conversation by chiming in with her own praise for the local schools, the food pantry, and some of her favorite library programs.

They managed to finish up their lunches without any further unpleasant conversation. Brinna and Tammy did all the talking, and it was a relief when Shirley announced she needed to get back to her office. The awkward group said their goodbyes, paid their bills, and Brinna breathed a huge sigh when she finally plopped down in the peace and quiet of Gabe's car.

"That was really uncomfortable," she announced to him when they were alone.

Gabe chuckled. "You're telling me. Wow, that Pete guy is a piece of work. What do you think he's really up to?"

"What?" Brinna gasped, feigning surprise. "You don't believe he's writing a book about old-time passenger rail in Ohio?"

"No, I most certainly do not."

She laughed. "He's not researching rural women in business, either, although he certainly got a lot of information from Tammy."

"That's not exactly hard to do," Gabe pointed out. "I can't help but notice that he's been looking into all the same things we have been. Boyston Industries, stories about that missing million dollars, the old factory site—"

"And don't forget he started with the railroad, specifically records from fifty years ago, not long before the railroad shut down."

"And we keep hearing that our missing Mr. Swenson left via passenger rail."

"That's just too many tie-ins," Brinna said. "You don't think he knows something about the murder, do you?"

"How could he? He's not from around here, and he's not even as old as our parents. I just don't see how there could be any connection."

"No, I can't figure it out, either. I've got a couple meetings at work this afternoon, but when I get a chance, I'll see what information I can find about Mr. Pete Snare the writer."

"If that's who he really is," Gabe added.

"You've been suspicious of him since the first day he came into the library," she mentioned. "Why is that?"

He shrugged, pulling the car into the light traffic on the main road going into town. "Cop intuition, maybe? Or maybe I just didn't like the way he swooped in on you, monopolizing your time for his personal research."

"So you think you're the only one who should get to do that, huh?"

"I never did that. I just… Yeah, okay, you're right. I did that. But there is something shady about the way *he* did it."

She laughed at him. "I'll certainly keep an eye on him if he comes back into the library."

"Call me. I'll come keep an eye on him for you."

"You've got a murder to solve, don't you? I can manage Pete Snare."

"I know you can. I just hope he doesn't actually need to be managed."

"You think he's dangerous?"

"I think he's deceitful, and that can definitely be dangerous."

She couldn't argue with that. "Don't worry, I'll be careful."

"The sooner we find some answers, the better I'll feel."

"About Pete Snare?" she asked.

"About everything."

Gabe dropped off Brinna at her grandfather's house so she could pick up her car and head into work. He called to check on his father and was happy to find him working on plans for a new Bible study he'd be offering in the fall. Kay was helping him type up the worksheets and plan the group activities. He sounded very excited about it. It was a whole study on the topic of God's grace.

Gabe was thrilled to hear the life coming back into his father's voice. After his stroke, he'd been so down and afraid to make plans for the future. The fact that he was working on this project now gave Gabe hope that he hadn't felt in quite a while. Hope for his father *and* for the church.

He offered up a prayer of thanks. There was so much to be grateful for in his life: his father's recovery, his own recovery from his previous injury, their ministry to the congregation, a job he loved with the police force, and now he had a fresh friendship with Brinna. His outlook on life had changed so much in just a few days. He would learn from this lesson. God's plans often come as a surprise, but they are always just what we need.

It was around one thirty when he arrived at the police station. He planned to do some searching on Pete Snare, making sure the guy didn't have a history they needed to know about. Instead, he found the station bustling and his chief summoning him.

"There you are," Chief Seigle said. "I know you're not scheduled to be here today, but I was just about to call you. You know I put in a request for the state GPR team to come check out that old factory site? Well, they were set for another job today, but it fell through. Rather than wasting the day, they're on their way here right now."

"Now? But we don't even have a warrant yet. We can't search the site."

The chief waved an envelope in Gabe's face. "Got the warrant ten minutes ago. I figured since you've been on this case since the start, you'd want to be there for the scan. You ready to head out?"

"Yes, sir."

Gabe ducked into the locker room and quickly put on his uniform. He collected his gear, jumped in his cruiser, and let dispatch know where he was headed. The GPR team from the state would probably be there by the time he arrived.

Realistically, the scan would probably turn up more questions than answers. They might detect nothing outside of the ordinary, or they might find signs of something buried in the earth, but that might not mean anything. The whole area had been disturbed by construction, and who knew what had been buried here and there over the years. The only way to know for sure if an anomaly was a body would be to dig it up.

Gabe prepared himself for the possibility that they might come up completely empty. He might end up no closer to the truth than he was the very day Mr. Kleinert made his confession—no evidence, no body, and no idea what really happened fifty years ago.

For now, he'd focus on following procedure. He wanted to call Brinna to tell her what was going on, but he couldn't. Chief Seigle had cautioned him that he didn't want a circus at the site. Only those who needed to know could be informed. People would find out soon enough. Shirley Boyston-Jones would probably not like the idea of them digging up the old factory site, and he expected there'd be quite an uproar in town.

When Gabe arrived at the site, he discovered there was a representative from Boyston Industries there. Ben Jenson. He knew his friend was unhappy with him for getting Brinna involved in this unpopular murder investigation, and he seemed really displeased to be overseeing a search for a possible grave site.

"I never thought you'd be the guy to take all those silly ghost stories we heard about as kids seriously, Gabe," Ben said as Gabe approached him.

He was standing with his arms crossed, watching as the radar team set up their equipment while investigators placed police tape and orange flags around the perimeter of their search area. Gabe was impressed by their efficiency.

"I'm not looking for ghosts today," Gabe said, standing beside Ben. "Our warrant says we're just here to run some invasive scans."

"You honestly think there's a body buried here? You're sure making a big deal out of everything. Do you have any idea how much of my time this is wasting? I'm standing around here when I've got a million things to get done back at my office."

"Then go back there, Ben. I know you're busy right now. There's nothing you can do here, anyway."

"Shirley wants me here. She says you were at lunch with her and never once mentioned this was going to happen. She thinks maybe I knew something about it."

"How could you? I didn't even know this was going on. I only found out when I went back to the station."

"Are you sure this whole thing isn't some excuse to manipulate Brinna into spending time with you?"

Gabe could hardly believe what he was hearing. "You think that's what this is? That I invented a murder investigation just to spend time with your sister?"

"I don't know what this is, just a big pain in the neck. You've stirred everything up and now I'm in a really hard place. My boss is grumpy, my in-laws are mad, and my fiancée isn't even sure she still wants my sister to be in our wedding because you've talked her into working with you! Do you know what kind of position that puts me in?"

"Brinna told me Zoey was upset with her, but I had no idea that—"

"Once again, you've got Brinna following you

around, looking up at you like some big hero, and she's going to end up hurt because of it."

"Ben, it's not like that at all."

He wanted to explain, to somehow make Ben see what was really going on, but one of the investigators called to him. He was needed. There was work to do, so he had to leave Ben to fume on his own.

Despite the personal ramifications of the case weighing on Gabe, the scan was a fascinating process. He'd worked with similar technology on a couple of projects during his time in the military. A grid was laid out, and a machine that looked something like a lawn mower with big wheels was pushed methodically over the grid. It was a slow process, but eventually, the area in question would all be scanned, and the data evaluated.

They were focusing on the area that was going to be the concrete floor of the factory at one time. Due to Gabe and Brinna's findings regarding the timing of the concrete's pour and the lack of financial records for it, Chief Seigle had agreed that the concrete floor was highly suspicious. If there was a body buried out here, it seemed most probable that the concrete had been poured over it.

For the next few hours, Gabe worked with the team. They made multiple passes over the area, focusing on a few places more than others as the scans indicated something of interest. The first scans were primarily to get an idea of what was beneath the huge concrete slab. As expected, there were all the indications of the soil being disturbed to a fairly standard depth by the construction. Once the "norm" had been determined, the scanner could be adjusted to pick up things that were outside those parameters.

At one point during the afternoon, Gabe noticed Shirley had joined Ben on-site. They talked quietly, but Gabe was in the middle of things and chose not to go to them. Ben had already made the company's viewpoint very clear, so there was no need to hear Shirley's version of it. Obviously, she was unhappy with this hassle, but there was nothing she could do about it.

If Shirley was so convinced there was not a body here, why was she still hovering around? And if she was here out of sheer curiosity, why didn't she let Ben leave to do the other important things he needed to do? Gabe couldn't help but wonder if they kind of expected something to turn up.

But, as the day dragged on, nothing did. The team slowly scanned every inch of the grid. Maybe it really was a waste of everyone's time. They were scanning a deeper depth now and finding fewer and fewer anomalies that needed analysis. It seemed there was nothing below the construction site besides good old Ohio farmland.

He watched as Shirley finally threw up her hands and got back into her Lexus and drove away. Ben stood around for a while longer, spending most of the time on his phone, then he eventually left, but not before he gave Gabe a meaningful glance full of warning and disapproval.

Gabe tried not to let it affect his attitude. The investigators and local officers on-site today were working hard. He owed it to them not to let his own frustrations carry over into how he did his job. When they said it was time to readjust some settings and tighten up their grid lines, he jumped in to help as needed.

He had long since digested that salad from lunch, and it was pretty obvious that everyone was getting tired and ready for dinner now. They'd followed a careful procedure all day and were in the final phases now. This current scan would be the last, then they would wait a few days before the analysis was complete.

Gabe was standing with the team at the table where a computer had been set up to view the scan in real time. The team leader was a woman named Jess. She'd been hunched over the screen all day but stepped back to stretch her sore muscles now.

"Looks like your guys are just about done," Gabe said to her.

"Yeah, just about," she agreed.

"Off the record, what do you think the chances are of your analysts recommending a more invasive investigation?" Gabe asked. He wasn't sure she would give him an answer, but it couldn't hurt to ask.

"Honestly?" she said. "Every anomaly that showed up could easily be explained as something natural or nonsuspicious. Judges don't like to give out warrants to make holes in private property, and police chiefs don't like to pay for heavy machinery, so I'd have to say it doesn't look like—"

A shout from one of the radar operators interrupted her. They all turned their focus back onto the computer screen. Gabe struggled to make sense of the various lines and strata that showed up, but murmurs from some of the others assured him that something unusual had shown up.

"Run over that bit again," Jess called out.

The team complied, and sure enough, the screen showed a distinct pattern of disruption in the lay of the soil. Gathering as much data as possible, the technicians and investigators were suddenly alive with interest. Gabe stepped back to let everyone work.

"They found something?" he asked Jess when there was a lull in activity.

"Yep, it's right there," she said, pointing to the

blurred and wavy lines on the screen. "That is a grave."

"You're sure of that?"

"On the record? No, I can't be sure of anything until we dig," she replied. "But off the record? Yeah, that's a grave. I've seen too many of them not to recognize one."

FOURTEEN

Brinna stifled another yawn and forced her attention back to the text displayed on a large screen at the front of the conference room. She was in the state capital, Columbus, Ohio, attending a day-long workshop hosted by the Heartland Preservation and Archival Guild. It was only ten o'clock in the morning, and the coffee she'd guzzled had done little to wake her up. Usually, she had no trouble engaging in these workshops, but today, her mind kept wandering. She'd stayed up way too late talking to Gabe on the phone last night.

He'd called her with exciting news—the scans at the old factory site had indeed picked up an anomaly that appeared to be a grave. The radar team recommended digging, and Gabe's chief had sent him directly to the judge to get a warrant. It was issued, and today the digging would begin.

It wasn't exactly good news to realize a murder had very likely occurred, but it did mean they were several important steps closer to solving this mystery. If this did turn out to be the victim Mr. Kleinert had mentioned, the real investigation could begin.

She and Gabe hadn't merely talked about the investigation, though. They talked about their lives, things they had done over the past ten years, and some of their hopes for the future. Brinna couldn't even remember how they'd gotten onto that subject, but it had felt so comfortable and natural talking to him about things that were important to her. He seemed to care, and he opened up to her about some of what he'd gone through with his injury and lengthy recovery.

She'd gone to bed thinking of Gabe, and now here she was, struggling to pay attention to a very good presentation about the best techniques for preserving old textiles. He promised he'd let her know what they found on-site today as soon as he could.

Of course, it wasn't fair to expect him to take time from his investigation to keep her informed of every little development. She wasn't a law enforcement agent, and he probably shouldn't tell her much of anything at this point. Still, she was eager to know what they'd dug up so far. And, if she was being honest with herself, she just wanted to hear from him.

She somehow made it through the rest of the textile session and breathed a sigh of relief when a fifteen-minute break was called. Checking her phone—again—she nearly squealed with delight when she discovered a text from Gabe had come in.

It looks like what we suspected. Won't know details for a while. Call me when you get a chance.

So, there really was a body buried there. She'd expected it, yet she was still surprised. To think something like this could've happened in peaceful New Minden, and that no one ever suspected. The poor guy—Barty, probably—got murdered and secretly buried, and no one had even noticed. It was hard to fully wrap her head around it.

Gabe wanted her to call him, so she hurried out to the hallway, found a quiet spot, and called. He answered right away.

"Hey, Brinna. Sorry, can't talk long. They're bringing the body up now. Looks like it's wrapped in some kind of plastic, so there's a possibility some evidence might be preserved."

"You've seen it?"

"I didn't get a good look, but yeah, it's definitely a body, and it definitely didn't put itself in that hole under the concrete."

"So it really was murder. Is it Barty Swenson?"

"We have to wait for the crime lab. They'll rely on DNA for identification."

"That means they need something to compare

it to," she noted. "Didn't Barty Swenson have a son? He'd probably give a sample. I'm sure I can find him for you."

"It's a police matter now. I've already started a search for the son but haven't found anything. It's like he just disappeared once he grew up."

"Hmm, maybe I can do some searching too, and then—"

"No, no need for that. Look, I've got to go now. I'll call you when we know something more. Until then, just enjoy your workshop and don't worry about this. I'll contact someone out in New Jersey and get them to help search for the son, okay?"

"Yeah, okay," she said.

She tried to sound cheerful as he dismissed her and said a hasty goodbye, and she didn't think he'd noticed his brush-off had hurt her. She hadn't expected him to keep talking to her when he had work to do there, but the way he'd cut her off felt needlessly harsh. After all the hours they'd worked on this together, it was painful to be told that her help was suddenly not needed.

She dropped her phone in her pocket and tried to shake it off. Gabe was just doing his job, and she needed to do hers. The library board had approved her participation in these quarterly workshops, so she owed it to them to learn something from her attendance. Feeling sorry for herself or second-guessing her shaky relationship with Gabe—whatever it was these days—was not what she was here for. Taking a deep breath, she shoved thoughts of the murder to the back of her mind and headed into the conference room to get ready for the next presentation.

After a quick glance at the day's agenda, she couldn't help but chuckle to herself. Maybe she should sit this one out, after all. It was called, How to Dig Up More Mystery in Your Own Backyard.

Gabe cringed as he disconnected the call to Brinna. He could tell she wasn't happy with his vague replies and his insistence she stay out of the investigation now. He wished he could've been honest with her, but it would've hurt her a lot more if he'd told her the truth of what they'd found.

There hadn't just been a body buried under that concrete. They'd found a gun. It was in rough condition after all this time, of course, but Gabe had seen it enough to recognize a revolver. He had no doubt that once the lab got hold of it, they'd be able to read the serial number, and he was pretty sure it was Brinna's grandfather's missing gun.

Gabe hadn't found the police report Mr. Randall said he'd filed when it was stolen weeks before the murder, so finding the gun here with the body didn't look good. If this turned out to be the murder weapon—and why else would it have been buried with the body?—investigators would have every reason to suspect the man who'd owned it. Mr. Randall would be in big trouble all over again, and a murder charge would be much worse than suspected embezzlement.

Gabe needed to tell Brinna. She deserved some sort of warning before it all came out in public, but she shouldn't have to hear this when she was an hour from home, sitting in some cold conference room surrounded by strangers. He wanted to tell her face-to-face here in New Minden, where he could assure her it was all going to be okay. But would it? If that gun did turn out to be her grandfather's, it would also mean Gabe would have to officially distance her from the case.

He wanted to protect Brinna for just a little while longer. If only he could protect her forever.

The lead investigator from the state crime team called to him. He needed to quit fretting over Brinna and get his mind back to his work. There was a body here that deserved proper treatment and careful investigation. This was a lot bigger than just his concerns for Brinna's feelings. A human being had been killed and buried here to be forgotten forever.

Gabe jogged back to the site to assist in whatever way he was needed. He breathed a quick prayer for the investigators to do their jobs carefully, and for the loved ones of the deceased to finally get closure after all these years. So many people would be affected by this.

Including Brinna.

Brinna tugged at her dress and hoped she didn't have lipstick on her teeth. It was Friday night, and she'd done her best to dress up for the big Boyston party. As expected, the ballroom at the corporate headquarters had been professionally decorated, and the caterer had provided top-notch food. Everyone around her seemed to be having a wonderful time, and Brinna hoped her false smile didn't dim anyone's joy.

She'd been out of sorts since her phone call with Gabe on Wednesday while she was at that conference. He'd been so short with her, obviously holding back information. It bothered her more than it should have, so she'd been short with him and claimed to be too busy to talk when he'd called again once she returned home. It was petty, of course, but she'd felt a wall come up between them, and that was a painful reminder of their past.

News of the body discovered at the old factory site had come out yesterday. It was the talk of the town. Everyone seemed to have an idea who it was and how they got there. Even Zoey had to acknowledge that Brinna and Gabe hadn't been stirring up trouble for no reason, but things were still quite tense. Not only was Zoey's grandfather still implicated in this mysterious death, but now Brinna's grandfather was, too.

She was furious with Gabe for not telling her right away about the gun that had been found. True, she hadn't given him a chance when he'd called again later, but at the time, it had seemed like avoiding him was the best idea, that it would somehow protect her heart or prove she wasn't really falling for him. She'd thought a couple of days away from him would make her less eager to see him again.

She'd been wrong. Very wrong. She didn't even know how it had happened. One minute she'd been calmly over him, the next minute she wasn't. And she had no reason at all to believe he felt the same.

So here she was, wearing her prettiest dress, wishing her curly hair would calm down just a bit, and blatantly staring at Gabe as he walked in through the wide glass doors. He looked good. He looked really good. He wore a dark gray suit with a crisp white shirt. What completed the look was the broad smile that spread across his face when his gaze caught on her.

She had to catch her breath. He waved at a

couple of people but made a beeline toward her. Frantically, she found a place to ditch her plate of messy hors d'oeuvres and quickly wiped her fingers. Now she hoped maybe there *was* lipstick on her teeth to cover up any spinach left there from the tiny quiches.

"Hi, Gabe," she greeted.

"Hello." His voice warm and hopeful. "I'm glad to see you, Brinna. I guess you got my messages?"

"Yes, I did," she acknowledged.

It had been rude of her not to call him back or at least text, but when the newspaper had come out yesterday with the story about the body and the gun that was found with it, she was too upset to talk to him. There'd been no details released about the gun yet, but she knew he couldn't have overlooked Grandpa's story about the gun that had been stolen from him.

"Look, Brinna… I wanted to talk to you before you read the papers, but—"

"It's okay." She cut him off before he apologized too much. "I get it. You tried to call me, and I brushed you off."

"Are you very upset with me?" He sounded worried.

She sighed and shook her head. "I was upset. I'm still upset, but not with you. It's not your fault that gun was in there. I wasn't going to be happy about it whether you told me or I read it in the newspaper. I was upset you told me to back out of the investigation, but I understand that, too. It's a police matter. I just wish I'd found something to keep my grandfather out of the whole mess."

He took a step toward her and lowered his voice. "Well, maybe I have some good news for you on that account."

This sounded promising, and she waited eagerly as he reached to pull out his phone, but they were interrupted. Tammy Crenshaw came bubbling up to them, gushing over the decorations, candles, and everyone's dressy attire.

"I'm just so happy everyone is having such a nice time," Tammy said. "I mean, this whole murder business isn't very pleasant, but it's wonderful to see everyone putting that aside and coming out tonight to celebrate our happy couple. What a generous thing for the Boystons to do this for them. Oh, here's Drexel now. I need to go tell him how nice everything is."

Without even waiting for Brinna or Gabe to comment, she floated away, calling to Drexel Boyston-Jones to force her conversation on him for a while.

Brinna shook her head. "I never quite know how to take her. But I guess it's good to see Drexel here. Sometimes I wonder if he has something against Ben."

"Oh? Why do you wonder about that?"

"It's the way Shirley makes such a big deal about Ben. It's like she's grooming him to take over the company for her, not Drexel, her own son. Don't you think that's a little bit odd?"

Gabe shrugged. "I don't know. Maybe Drexel doesn't want to be in charge? He's got to be fifty years old by now. Maybe he's already thinking of retirement. Just because Shirley wants to keep working in her seventies doesn't mean her son wants to."

"True. I guess it doesn't matter. He seems like he's happy enough for Zoey and Ben."

"Who wouldn't be? Just look at them, all smiles. Did you and Zoey patch things up? Ben mentioned she was angry about you helping investigate her grandfather."

"Well, we're on speaking terms, at least. She still wants me in her wedding, and she did say she realizes the investigation wasn't anything personal. I think we'll get through this and be best friends again, eventually. She's got a lot to process right now."

"Which brings me back to my news for the day," he said, pulling out his phone again. "I probably shouldn't show you this, but I think you have a right to know. They found the murder weapon, and it wasn't the gun."

She had to grab the nearby table to catch herself. "What? It wasn't the gun?"

"No, it was this."

He held his phone out so she could look at it. There was a photo of an object on a metal table, probably in the autopsy room at the state crime lab. She tried to forget that and focus on the object in the photo.

It appeared to be a knife—no, not a knife. There was no handle. It seemed to have been broken off. The other end of the object was very pointed and about eight inches long. It wasn't flat like a knife, though. It was round and twisted.

"Is it a piece of rebar?" she asked.

"That's what I thought, but no. It's too…finished, like it's a piece of something. The examiner isn't sure what it is, but it was embedded in the man's chest. It must've gone right through his heart. He probably died instantly."

"So he wasn't shot. Wow." She paused for a moment to comprehend. Even if the gun found in the grave turned out to be Grandpa's, it wasn't the murder weapon. That was good news.

"They're still going to trace the serial number on the gun," he said. "So if it was the one stolen from your grandfather, that will come out, but at least no one can say he committed murder with it."

"That's wonderful. Maybe Barty was the one

who stole the gun all along. Thank you for telling me, Gabe. I really appreciate it."

"You'll have to keep quiet about it for a little while."

"I will. The last thing I want to do is stir things up any more than they are already or get you in trouble. How is the investigation going? Is the chief still letting you run the show?"

"I'm still the lead, but it's all in the hands of the Ohio Bureau of Criminal Investigation, really. They'll issue the final ID."

"Any hints on that? Do you think it might be who we suspected?"

He glanced around, clearly nervous about giving out too much information. "It's a man—that much we know. We're just waiting for the DNA results."

"How long will that take? Any clues on where to find the missing son to get a sample for comparison?"

He cleared his throat, and his voice became nearly inaudible. "He turned up. We got the sample. They're running it now."

She was floored. "What?! How did you find him?"

"Shhh, no one can know about this. He turned up, that's all I can say."

As it turned out, it really *was* all he could say. Some friends from high school came over to catch up. Brinna was forced to abandon her questions for Gabe and pretend to be just another partygoer having a nice time. After a few minutes, she realized she wasn't having to pretend.

She was having a nice time. They laughed, reminisced about things they'd done as kids, and looked at everyone's photos of children, pets, and recent vacations. All talk of murder and scandal faded away, and they were all just friends again, remembering the good times and reveling in each other's achievements.

Shirley and her family even stopped by to check in with the group. She introduced everyone to her husband, Renner, and her son, Drexel, and thanked them all for coming. Brinna had half feared someone from Boyston might accuse Gabe of causing trouble with the investigation, but no one did, so the laughter continued.

At one point, Shirley got a text and excused herself from the group. Drexel and Renner stayed to chat a bit more, then Ben came along and joined them. Soon, Ben's high school friends were telling stories about him to his current bosses, which led to more laughter and lighthearted ribbing. Ben seemed to really enjoy the attention.

Brinna began looking around, trying to catch Zoey's eye. She should be in this conversation, cutting up with their old group. If anyone knew how to tease Ben, it was Zoey, and she was missing out on a golden opportunity here. Finally, Brinna found her in the crowd.

They made eye contact. At first, Zoey glanced away, but then she looked back, and Brinna motioned to her. She could tell Zoey wasn't quite ready to forgive and forget, but Brinna missed her. If there was anything she could do to smooth things over, she would do it.

Excusing herself from the group, she started toward her best friend. Zoey had been caught in conversation with Tammy Crenshaw and a couple of other Boyston employees who Brinna didn't really know well, so she figured this might be a good time to step in. Zoey might still be mad at her, but surely she'd appreciate being rescued from Tammy.

"Sorry to interrupt," Brinna began, "but Ben's trying to tell us about the honeymoon plans, and I think he's messing it all up. Is there any way you can come over and set things straight, Zoey?"

The other ladies agreed that Zoey should certainly head off with Brinna, so she graciously agreed. Brinna hoped this had been the right tactic and that she hadn't succeeded in upsetting Zoey even more.

"Thank you," Zoey said, setting her mind at ease. "I've been trying to get away for the past ten minutes."

"It's nice that they care about you," Brinna

said. "I just thought Ben could use some moral support right now."

"Oh? Why's that?" Zoey asked.

Brinna pointed at the loud group she'd just left. "Gabe, Tyler Poston, and Chuck Ross are reciting Ben's most embarrassing teenage moments to Renner and Drexel Boyston-Jones."

"Oh no." Zoey sighed, shaking her head. She then gave Brinna a devious grin. "I absolutely need to be in on this conversation. They'll probably skip over all the good parts."

Brinna laughed, and they joined the group. As expected, Zoey dominated the conversation, and Ben groaned with humor as she amended the stories his friends had been telling. For the next few wonderful minutes, it was as if nothing bad had ever happened, as if Gabe hadn't gone away, as if Zoey hadn't lost her grandfather and gotten angry with Brinna, and as if a murdered man had not just been dug up two days ago.

Brinna was enjoying her evening so much that she very nearly missed hearing her phone buzz in her small handbag. When she finally noticed, she checked quickly to find there were three texts. What she couldn't understand was that they were all from Ben's phone.

"Hey," she said to her brother. "I keep getting texts from you. Is your phone dialing me from your pocket or something?"

Ben shrugged and dug in his pocket for his phone, then he rolled his eyes and showed empty hands.

"I don't have my phone," he said. "Shirley took it from me. She said I needed to stop looking at it and just have a good time tonight."

"And I love her for that," Zoey said. "She's right, you need to forget about work every now and then, Mr. Jenson. Tonight is about ignoring the phone and having fun."

Brinna wasn't the only one who'd been checking her phone. She noticed Renner and Drexel had their phones in their hands, and they looked just as perplexed as Brinna.

"Is Ben's phone texting you as well?" she asked them.

"No, it's a security alert," Renner said, glancing at his son. "You got one, too?"

Drexel nodded. "Someone's in the offices. They shouldn't be up there now."

"Probably just someone from the party," Ben said.

"Whoever it is," Brinna said, "they want me to come up there."

Gabe leaned over to look at Brinna's phone. "Who sent those?"

"It's from Ben's phone, but the texts say they're from Shirley."

She showed Gabe the messages and also read

them aloud for the others. "The first one says, 'It's Shirley. Come to my office ASAP. Urgent.' The second one says, 'Now!' and the third one is just exclamation points."

"Why would Shirley text you on my phone?" Ben asked.

"I have no idea," Brinna said.

"I think we'd better get up there," Renner said. His son agreed.

"If it's a security issue, maybe I should come along, too," Gabe said.

"Well, I'm the one she asked for," Brinna pointed out.

"And she's got my phone," Ben said.

"Sounds like we're all going up to the offices," Zoey said.

Gabe didn't approve of that idea, of course, but they were already leaving the party and heading toward the wide staircase that led up to the second floor, the younger ones dashing up a little faster than the two older men. Renner and Drexel weren't dawdling, though. It was clear they were concerned.

Brinna was, too. Something strange was going on, and based on how the rest of the week had gone, she couldn't even guess what it might be. The one thing she did know was that Gabe was right by her side, and she liked it that way.

FIFTEEN

Gabe continued to be impressed by Brinna's courage, but he wished she would've stayed downstairs. Something about this just didn't feel right, and he'd been in enough dangerous situations to know to trust his gut. Right now, his gut was telling him Brinna was being lured up here for some reason that didn't include another tray of finger foods and cheerful conversation.

What was Shirley up to? With all the details of this murder about to become public knowledge, and Boyston Industries being caught in the middle of it, the aging CEO might be desperate to hide things from the past. But how did Brinna figure into that? Gabe could think of no comforting scenario.

"Where's her office?" Gabe asked when they reached the reception area at the top of the stairs.

"Down there." Ben pointed. "The door at the end of the hallway."

"But that room is dark," Brinna said. "Light

seems to be coming from that area over there, though, off to the side."

"The executive conference room," Ben said, leading the way.

Sure enough, the only light spilling into the hallway came from an alcove with double doors that were open wide. The long conference table inside was ringed by executive chairs, and the room was furnished with cabinetry from the company's manufacturing history. One whole wall was devoted to trophies and awards that had been earned over the years. Clearly, the Boyston executives liked to be reminded of the past. Gabe, however, was more interested in right now. Low voices indicated someone was inside the room, just out of sight.

Gabe held up his hand to warn the group to be cautious. He had no idea what they were walking into, and he didn't like it. He positioned himself in front of the others and moved silently through the doorway.

He could see Shirley at the far end of the room. She was with a man, Pete Snare, and this time he was wearing a familiar ballcap. That was a surprise. The two of them were in tense conversation—his voice low and threatening, hers raspy and anxious. They seemed to be working at something, and Gabe took advantage of their distraction to assess the situation.

The pair were leaning over a cabinet. No, not

a cabinet; it was an old safe. Pete was actively working at the lock while Shirley watched over his shoulder. She shifted nervously.

"You must be doing it wrong," she hissed.

"It hasn't been used in years. It's rusty," Pete replied.

"Maybe that isn't the right combination," she suggested. "I'll go see if I can find—"

"You'll stay here," Pete demanded. "The combination *has* to be right. This is the same safe that's in the old photo I found. Why would it have the wrong combination written on the back?"

"I don't know why you're so determined to open it. I already told you that—"

Gabe was hoping the others would stay safely out in the hallway, but of course, Brinna had followed him into the room, and now the others crowded in the doorway as well. They weren't quiet about it, either. Shirley and Pete stopped what they were doing and turned in shock to find an audience. Pete didn't seem thrilled at their arrival, but Shirley breathed a sigh of relief.

"Renner! Drexel! I'm glad you're here."

"What's going on?" Renner asked. "Are you trying to open that old safe?"

Shirley took a step away from Pete and pointed an accusing finger at him. "He is. He's convinced it's full of old money."

"*Stolen* money," Pete corrected, glaring at her.

"And don't act like you don't know anything about it. You were around then. You know about my father's million dollars."

There was a distinct silence after his words.

Suddenly, Brinna exclaimed, "Pete Snare isn't your real name. You're Barty Swenson's son from New Jersey! Of course, that's how they got a DNA sample." Before Pete could reply, she whirled on Gabe. "Did you actually know about this?"

"I found out just before the party," he defended quickly. "I got the message, but I wasn't at liberty to discuss it. Sorry, Brinna. I would've told you as soon as I could."

Shirley jumped into the conversation. "There's a DNA match? You ran DNA tests? And no one from the police contacted us?"

Gabe took a deep breath. "It's an ongoing investigation. Information will be made public when it's appropriate to—"

But no one was listening to Gabe's explanation. Renner rushed over to Shirley and reassured her that he'd sort this all out for her. Drexel seemed confused by everything and was peppering Gabe with questions. Pete backed away from the safe, glancing around the room as if he might need to make a hasty exit. Gabe stayed near the door to make sure that didn't happen. Brinna, however, stepped farther into the room and seemed determined to put all the pieces together without any help from Gabe.

"You didn't come here to research trains, did you, Mr. Snare? I guess I should call you Mr. Swenson. I ran across your name while I was researching your father. It's, um, Porter, isn't it? Porter Swenson."

Pete seemed flattered that she would know that. "Yes, that's right. My real name is Porter Swenson, and my father was Barty. I'm not writing a book about trains—sorry I lied to you—but I *was* looking for information about trains. The last thing anyone remembers about my father was that he got two train tickets out of town. Everyone says he left with a woman. You kindly educated me on train schedules and those amazingly detailed ticket records you have, and I thought maybe I could figure out where they were going. Instead, I found out he had a million dollars."

"But if he left, he must have taken his money with him," Shirley offered, "Why do you think it's still in this old safe?"

"Because when I asked you about the money and the rumors I'd heard about an old safe at the factory, you flat out denied it. You laughed at me for listening to ghost stories. You said there was no safe and no million dollars. Well, here's the safe, and I saw Brinna's notes that mentioned an article confirming the million dollars. So I know it's real, and you're just trying to keep me from it. I went back to the library after hours and did some more poking around."

"You broke into my office! You're the one who took that old photo," Brinna said. "You assumed the numbers written on the back were the combination to the safe in the photo."

"And this is the same safe. But it's not working," Pete complained. "Shirley said everything from the old building had been brought here, and Tammy talked about the big party tonight, so I knew these offices would be empty. I let myself in and had a go at it. When it didn't work, I brought Shirley up here to help me. Once I told her who I am and hinted I might have some information she wouldn't want to be made public, she decided to be very helpful."

"You still haven't got the thing open, I notice," Gabe mentioned.

"No. I don't understand why. But I'm not leaving until I find out if my father's money has been hidden here all this time while he's been lying dead."

"Don't be ridiculous," Renner said, protectively putting his arm around his wife. "If there ever was a million dollars, do you really think we'd have just left it sitting around? No, your father must've taken it when he left. As you said yourself, there are credible accounts of him buying a train ticket and leaving with a woman."

"Then why did my DNA match the body they pulled up from under that concrete?" Pete asked. "Yes, I went to the police station and told them who I am. They took my DNA sample to the crime lab, and I got a text with the results just a couple hours ago. That dead man *is* Barty Swenson, my father. Now, if one of you Boystons will be nice enough to help me find my million dollars, I won't insist on finding out which one of you killed him."

"Well, *I'm* going to find out," Gabe interrupted. "And I'm going to ask you to step away from the safe and show me your hands, Pete—or whatever your name is."

"Porter Swenson," Brinna said under her breath.

"Thank you," Gabe said with a sigh. "I understand you want answers, Swenson, and you surely deserve them. If there is a million dollars, you probably deserve that too, but making threats and demands isn't the way to go about it. Shirley, can you tell me what the combination to this safe actually is?"

"No, I can't," she said. "It's been lost for as long as I can remember. There's nothing in it, though. We installed it at the new site back then, but it was never used. Once the project was abandoned, we hauled anything of value back to headquarters. This safe sat in storage for years and years, until we built this new facility and brought it up here as a decorative antique. We serve doughnuts and coffee on it now."

"You've never opened it?" Gabe asked.

Shirley shook her head, and Renner answered for her. "We called in an expert to open it once, but without the combination he said he'd have to cut into it. Since it's empty anyway, we decided not to ruin the aesthetic value and told him not to bother. So here it sits, useless."

Brinna moved toward them, her eyes fixed on the safe. Gabe was still uncertain about how far he could trust Porter Swenson, so he followed her. The others came along after him, all moving in to get a better look at the old, forgotten safe.

"Let me see the photo you stole from the library," Brinna said, reaching her hand out toward Porter.

He made a face, but after a brief hesitation, he pulled the photo out of his pocket. Brinna took it carefully, smoothing it out and turning it over to read the back. Gabe leaned in to see the series of four numbers on the back. It certainly did look like a combination.

"It doesn't work, though," Porter insisted.

"It's obvious this is just a waste of time," Shirley said. "I can't believe we're up here while there's a perfectly nice party downstairs."

"Wait," Brinna said. "These are the numbers you were trying?"

"Yes," Porter replied.

"They aren't the right ones," Brinna announced.

Shirley snorted. "Obviously! He's wasting everyone's time with this. The safe is empty, there's no million dollars, and I don't know anything about his father. Aren't the police handling that? We should let them. Tonight is supposed to be about Ben and Zoey. Let's go downstairs and forget about all this right now."

"Or we could try another combination and see if the safe really *is* empty," Brinna said.

"You know another combination?" Gabe asked.

Brinna smiled at him. "No, but I think I know why this one isn't working."

Brinna knew Gabe wasn't happy with this situation. He seemed very tense where Porter Swenson and his veiled threats were concerned, and since all of this was tied to his investigation, he probably would've preferred to usher everyone out and seal this up as a possible crime scene. But no crime had been committed here. This building hadn't even been built when Barty Swenson was killed. Besides, they all wanted to know what was in the safe. She watched Gabe with hopeful eyes and waited until he finally nodded for her to continue.

"All right, Brinna," he said. "Explain to us why you think you can get into the safe."

"My grandfather was in charge of this safe when it was first installed in the new factory. This is a photo of him with the safe in the background, and these numbers are in his handwriting," she said, holding up the photo so the others could see. "It was a new safe, so he probably wrote the combination down until he had it memorized. He certainly wouldn't want an unauthorized person to open it."

"So why didn't that combination work?" Zoey asked.

Ben broke into laughter. "It's Grandpa's code," he exclaimed.

Brinna nodded enthusiastically. "It's got to be. Come on, help me with this."

Ben quickly pushed past the others and made his way to Brinna's side. They went to the safe, and Brinna consulted the numbers on the back of her old photo while Ben dutifully worked the dial on the lock. Gabe was at a loss, but they both seemed to know exactly what to do.

Brinna read the numbers one at a time. Ben thought for a moment, then moved the dial in a calculated manner. They did this four times for four numbers, then Ben pulled at the handle to open the safe.

Nothing happened.

"I have no idea what numbers you were using, but on that last turn, you needed to go around the dial one whole turn, then come back to the number," Porter informed Ben. "I think you missed that part."

Ben shrugged. "I'm not really an expert at cracking old safes."

"Let me try," Porter said, pushing Ben aside.

"I stayed up half the night studying this on the internet. Tell me the code you're using, and I can get the door open."

"Okay," Brinna agreed. "It's a thing my grandpa does, and you'd better not let him know I've told you about it."

She explained Grandpa's code, and Porter followed along.

"It's that simple?" he asked, surprised. "Okay then, let's give it a try."

Brinna read the numbers again, adding and subtracting as needed to give Porter what she hoped were the right numbers. He seemed to understand how to turn the dial, whether to the right or the left, and on the fourth number, she could practically hear them all hold their breath as Porter reached for the handle.

It opened. And just as Shirley had said, it was empty.

She leaned over Brinna's shoulder. "See? Just as I told you."

"If you were so sure, why did you look inside?" Brinna asked.

"So where is the million dollars?" Porter questioned. "I thought for sure it would be in there."

"There is no million dollars," Shirley said firmly. "I keep telling you that. I know you've heard all the silly rumors, but believe me, there never was a million dollars."

"But the article said my father was an investor and—"

"He lied about that," Shirley announced. "He lied about a lot of things. That's what he did, he was a liar and a con artist. He came here and duped us all, the whole family. My father took out loans and spent money he didn't have because he trusted your father. In the end, it was all a big fat lie, and we nearly went under because of it. Okay?"

Porter clearly wanted to discuss these points, but Brinna cut in before he could speak.

"I thought it was supposed to be my grandfather who nearly bankrupted the company," she said. "Now you're blaming Barty Swenson?"

"Is that why someone killed him?" Porter asked.

Shirley was flustered in the face of these questions. She sputtered a bit and tried to explain herself, but she was cut off when Zoey interrupted.

"Wait! Look down there." Zoey pointed to the inside of the safe.

Brinna didn't see anything at first, but then she noticed that one corner of the metal floor inside the safe was slightly off to the side, and the tiniest hint of something white was showing. It looked like paper.

Brinna and Gabe both stooped in at the same time. They shared a quick smile, and he reached into the safe to touch the anomaly. He followed the edge of the black metal, and the whole thing shifted. He worked his fingers under it and lifted it up.

"A false bottom!" Brinna gasped.

There was a very shallow area below the black metal sheet. The white they'd seen turned out to be papers that spilled out of a manila folder. Gabe held the black metal up with one hand and retrieved the folder with the other. He brought it out into the light.

"That's not a million dollars," Porter noted.

Gabe opened the folder, and Brinna scanned the top page inside. It took a few moments to realize what she was looking at, but her brother was standing over her, and he let out a long, slow breath.

"This is a transfer ledger from fifty years ago," Ben said. "It lists transfers that just happen to add up to the amount that our grandfather is accused of embezzling."

"Oh, how can you be sure of that?" Shirley said dismissively. "Those are just some old papers that got jammed in there."

Gabe handed the folder to Ben. With his background in business, he barely had to glance at the pages to interpret them. With wide eyes, he gave Brinna a huge grin.

"I've studied the ledgers from that time, hoping to find something to clear Grandpa's name, but these aren't the same numbers listed in the official ledgers. Those must have been doctored. These are the originals, and they show where the money really went." He turned to his boss, and his expression was much less exuberant. "Shirley, the money wasn't stolen, it was moved into your father's accounts hidden at other banks."

"That's not possible, Ben." Shirley said, her surprise almost believable...*almost*. "These aren't anything at all, just old pages. You know I would love to prove your grandfather's innocence, but—"

"Then do it, Shirley. These statements will prove it, and someone knew that. They were hidden in here for a reason, probably to implicate my grandfather. I assure you, though, my grandfather would've been the first person to bring these out if he'd known about them. Did you know about them, Shirley? Did you transfer all the money and claim it had been stolen?"

"Me? No, I was still in college. I didn't have any authority to do that," Shirley insisted.

"Then who did?" Gabe asked.

Shirley slumped against Renner. She took a deep breath and stared up at the ceiling for a moment while she seemed to gather her thoughts. Whether she was fabricating a fanciful excuse or preparing herself for a confession, Brinna could hardly wait to find out.

"It was my father," Shirley said at last. "But we didn't know about it until years later. We learned the truth after he died and my mother had to sort everything out. Ben, I'm so sorry. I should've spoken up and defended your grandfather, but by then, it was all water under the bridge. Mom and I made it up to your family, didn't we? Look at you, poised to be a top executive here someday."

Ben simply shook his head in dismay. Zoey stood close to him and took his hand. Brinna had to push her own emotions off to the side for now. The injustice done to her family was all just a part of a much larger picture that was wrapped up in murder.

"Did Barty Swenson know what your father had done?" Brinna asked Shirley. "Did he try to blackmail him over it? Is that why he was murdered?"

Shirley shook her head. "No, my father never knew what happened to Barty."

Shirley's son, Drexel, had remained a few paces away from the group, leaning against the wall next to the proud display of trophies and awards. He was a middle-aged man, yet he folded his arms and glared like a sullen teenager.

"So Boyston Industries is rotten to the core. I should've known, Mother. To think, all this time I worried you didn't want me in the business because you thought I wasn't good enough. Really, you were just afraid of what I might find out."

"No, Drexel. It isn't like that..." Shirley began.

"Then what is it like?" Drexel demanded. "It's

all built on a lie. You convinced me that Grandmother was a genius for saving the company after Grandfather died, but she simply found the money he'd stashed in secret accounts. It wasn't some imaginary million dollars that saved our family, or even Dad's money when you married him. It was our own money that Grandma used, and she didn't bother to come clean about where it had come from."

"Drexel, it would've only caused more damage if we had told people about it. The important thing at the time was to maintain stability, to keep people's trust."

"So they wouldn't ask questions, Mother? So they wouldn't find out that someone had been murdered?"

"He wasn't murdered," Shirley shouted.

Renner tried to calm her, to keep her from saying more. Most of the group was stunned into silence. Was Shirley still denying that Barty's body had been discovered, or did she know more about the death?

"How *did* he die, Shirley?" Gabe demanded. "Maybe it's time for you to tell us about it."

SIXTEEN

Renner still had his arm wrapped around Shirley. "She has nothing to say. She doesn't know anything."

Brinna had no idea what Shirley did or didn't know about Barty's death, but one look at Renner's face told her that he, at least, knew something about it. She glanced over to Drexel. Was he aware that his parents were in on a murder? Or was this another secret his family had been keeping from him?

As she watched him, her eye caught on the trophies in the long glass cabinet beside him. They glinted proudly in the overhead lighting, accolades for the many Boyston achievements over the years. The collection of Singularity Awards stood out in particular, one whole shelf of them. She remembered how proud Carolyn was of the community service and philanthropy that had earned them those awards. She used to keep the newest award proudly displayed on her own private desk. It was impressive to see the sleek unicorn shapes all lined up this way—all but the one that had been donated to the archives, of course. The one that was broken.

Then, like a bolt of electricity through her, Brinna understood.

"Gabe, show me that picture on your phone again," she said quickly.

He seemed confused, so she nodded her head toward the glass cabinet. He wrinkled his brow for a moment, then he pulled out his phone and brought up the photo he'd shown her earlier. Sure enough, the murder weapon that had been found lodged in the dead man's chest was a match.

"The unicorn horn," Gabe murmured under his breath.

"What?" Shirley said, craning her neck to see. "What are you talking about?"

"Barty Swenson died in the old Boyston offices, didn't he?" Brinna asked. "In your mother's office, in fact."

Shirley looked stunned.

"Yes! It was Carolyn, all right?" Renner admitted, his words coming rapidly. "She found out that Barty had lied about the money, so she killed him. Shirley had nothing to do with it. She didn't even know Barty Swenson."

"But she *did* know him," Brinna corrected. "She was home from college that summer, and

people saw him flirting with her. She told us herself that he duped the *whole* family. How could
he do that if she didn't even know him?"

"She's right, Shirley," Gabe said with a deep
finality to his voice. "We've got the murder
weapon, and we know how he was killed. You
might as well tell us the details. Did your mother
kill Barty Swenson?"

"No," Shirley said firmly. "It was an accident,
and my mother had nothing to do with it. I was
the only one with him at the time. It's true. I met
Barty while I was home that summer. I knew
him, and I was there when he died."

Renner's voice cracked as he tried to advise
his wife. "You don't have to do this, Shirley. Let
me call our lawyer."

But she brushed him off. "No, Renner. You
don't need to protect me anymore. Gabe's right.
It *is* time for me to talk about this."

"If you'd like to have your lawyer present, that
might not be a bad idea," Gabe said. "We can go
down to the station, and you can make a formal
statement there."

"I will." Shirley sighed. "But Drexel deserves
to hear it from me first. If you don't mind, I'll
just tell you about it now. Then we can go and
make it formal."

Gabe nodded. "All right. Let's hear it."

"Barty was a con man," Shirley began. "My

father was looking for an investor to help get the new factory project off the ground, and Barty seemed to fit the bill. He came in with all sorts of promises, so my father gave him the red-carpet treatment—fancy meals, and all expenses paid. Barty took advantage of that. What my father didn't know was that I had also fallen for Barty's lies. Yes, he flirted with me, and I thought he actually cared. I didn't realize until it was too late that none of it was real."

"You had a thing with my father?" Porter asked.

"You don't have to tell any of this," Renner said, clutching Shirley's hand.

Shirley gave him a sad smile. "I want to tell. We've kept the secrets too long, Renner. It's time for the truth."

She told them how she'd fallen under Barty's spell when she was home on summer break, and how they'd kept seeing each other secretly even after she'd gone back to college. Work continued on the new factory, and Clement Boyston trusted Barty's claims of wanting to invest. In fact, he began embezzling money from the company to put it in his own private accounts, planning to use Barty's money to hide it. But Barty's money never materialized and Boyston Industries couldn't meet payroll one week.

"Is that when everyone found out Boyston Industries was nearly broke?" Gabe asked.

"Yeah," Shirley said. "My dad knew there was trouble, that's why he started embezzling to begin with. I guess he figured if he hid the money, then we'd be okay even if the company failed."

"If he could sneak money away from the company, why didn't he just sneak it back in when it all fell apart?" Brinna asked.

"I think it was because Barty was blackmailing him," Shirley explained. "I was at school when the financial troubles started, and my parents hid it from me at first. Poor Dad…he really trusted Barty, but then Barty figured out what he did and insisted on a contract giving him ownership in the company, or else he'd blow the whistle."

"Ownership?" Porter said. "Does that mean I inherited part of Boyston Industries?"

Shirley shook her head. "No. My father ripped up that contract the day I came home to tell him about me and Barty…and that I was pregnant."

A ripple of audible surprise ran through the room.

Drexel nearly choked when he spoke. "Mother! You can't mean that Barty Swenson is actually my father?"

"I'm sorry." Shirley sighed. "I thought you'd never have to find out. Renner and I always wanted you, even if Barty didn't. He just laughed when I told him I was expecting. He didn't want me…or my child. It was the first time he admitted he already had a wife and child. That's when it happened…when he died."

"Did your father have something to do with that?" Gabe asked. "Did he kill him because of the blackmail?"

"No, it truly was an accident," Shirley insisted. "I had no idea about the embezzlement or the blackmail. When Barty rejected me, I thought maybe if I told my father about my situation, he could make Barty marry me. He called Barty in to see him, and that's when he tore up that contract and told Barty to get out of town. I didn't see Barty again until later, when he came into my mother's office to demand his final expense check. It was after hours and I was the only one there. I begged him not to abandon me, but he said he was leaving."

"If he was leaving you, why did he have two train tickets?" Gabe asked.

"He didn't. It wasn't Barty who bought tickets that night."

"It was me," Renner said. "Shirley and I had known each other forever. Our parents were good friends, and they'd been trying to get us together since we were teenagers. Of course, we were too rebellious for that, so we were always just friends. When Clement found out about Shirley, he was desperate to push us together. He came up with some excuse to invite me down for the weekend, and I arrived in New Minden just in time to find out what had happened. I helped Shirley by buying tickets in Barty's name and taking the train with her that night. If you had eyewitnesses that claimed they saw him leaving with a woman, it's because we intentionally made it look that way."

Shirley smiled at him and squeezed his hand. "You never batted an eye, despite the horrible spot I was in. How could I not fall in love with you after that?"

Renner chuckled and finished the story for the rest of the group. "We left that night. We went back to college so she'd have a solid alibi, and we eloped a couple weeks later. I regret all the lies and what happened to Barty, but I've never regretted marrying Shirley Boyston."

Drexel grumbled to himself. "This is a lot to take in."

Porter heartily agreed. "Yeah, I'm glad there was a happy ending for you guys, but what about my father? When did you get around to killing him?"

"I didn't kill him," Shirely repeated. "We argued in my mother's office. He laughed at me and called me horrible names, so I told him I would contact his wife. That made him furious, and he pulled a gun on me—said it was just one of the many things he'd stolen from the company. I was terrified and pushed him away…that's when he fell."

"He *fell*?" Porter questioned dubiously.

"He fell against my mother's desk," Shirley clarified.

"And that's where she kept her Singularity Award, isn't it?" Brinna asked.

Shirley nodded, but most of the others looked around in confusion.

"One of those," Gabe said, pointing to the row of distinctly shaped awards in the trophy cabinet. "The examiner found one of those unicorn horns embedded in the chest of the corpse. We have that piece of evidence as well as the award that it was broken off of all those years ago. We can prove that it came from Carolyn Boyston's possessions, so the story holds up."

"He fell onto the award," Shirley confirmed. "It was terrible. There was so much blood. I started screaming, and I guess my mother was still in the building, because she was suddenly there with Dwight Kleinert. We tried to help Barty, but it was too late. He died right there in front of us. I wanted to call the police, but Dwight suggested there might be a better way. He convinced my mother that this sort of thing would be very bad for the company, that with the financial trouble and the investigation, something like this could ruin us. So Mom did what she always did and put the company first. She sent Dwight off to take care of Barty's body and the gun, and we got busy cleaning the office. At some point, Renner showed up, and you know what happened then."

"All this happened after the scandal about the money?" Brinna asked.

"The construction had been shut down for a few days," Shirley answered. "Dwight buried Barty there because it was all ready for concrete to be poured. I never even thought about it at the time, but I guess my mother must've ordered the concrete at a later date, just to be sure no one would find out what had happened."

"The fact that the concrete came at a later date is actually what tipped us off that there might be something suspicious under it," Gabe informed her.

"That figures," she said with a sigh. "My father never told us about all the money he had hidden and that was probably because we didn't tell him about Barty. He thought he was still alive out there somewhere and was going to blackmail him again. I don't think my father was brave enough to touch that money, even when it looked like the company would go bankrupt. That's probably why he had his heart attack so soon after all that."

"Lies never make things better," Gabe said. "Is there anything else you need to tell us, Shirley?"

She slumped, giving a deep sigh of relief. "No. I think that's all of it, except…except that I'm really sorry. You lost your father, Pete—I mean, Porter—and you shouldn't have had to wait all these years to find out how."

"I'm glad to finally know the truth, even though I was hoping for a happier ending," Porter said. "I wish my mother had lived long enough to find out that my father didn't actually leave her. He probably would've come home to us."

"I think he would have," Shirley said with a touch of sadness. "I can't say he was a good man, but he didn't want me because he already had a family. I just hope you can forgive me for my part in your loss."

"I'll work on that," Porter said. "In the meantime, I guess I should go over and shake hands with the little brother I never knew I had."

Renner slapped his son on the back. "Drexel is the best thing to come out of all of this. I hope you won't think me any less of a father for keeping the truth from you all these years, but you've never been anything other than my own son."

"Thanks, Dad," Drexel said, "but I'm nearly fifty years old. It's not like I could start thinking of you as anything other than my father, so you're stuck with that. As for having a brother, I guess I could get used to that."

It was touching to see Drexel and Porter meeting each other for the first time and witnessing Shirley and Renner giving up the heavy burden they'd carried for so long. Brinna couldn't help but smile as she watched the people around her reacting to this new reality they suddenly found themselves in. She glanced at Zoey and Ben and realized that not everyone was feeling so warm and fuzzy.

"Are you all right, Zoey?" she asked.

"No," Zoey exclaimed. Then she shook her head, straightened her dress, and took a deep breath. "We're all going to be unpacking this for a long, long time, Brin. But we'll help each other through it, won't we? We are not going to let the Boyston scandal ruin our friendship."

Brinna beamed at her friend. They *were* going to get through this. She gave a quick glance over to Gabe, and he smiled.

"You guys go back downstairs," he directed. "I'll take Shirley and Renner to the station for their official statements, but we don't need to make a big deal about it. For now, enjoy the party like nothing happened."

"Are you going to arrest me?" Shirley asked.

"We'll just get your statements for now," Gabe assured her. "But I can't promise there won't be charges filed at some point."

"I understand," Shirley said. She gave a feeble smile to her husband and son and then turned to

Brinna. "I'm sorry for not doing anything to help your grandfather," she said. "I have failed a lot of people, and I wish I could change that."

Brinna couldn't help but feel sorry for the woman, despite all the things she'd confessed to. She tried to imagine herself as a traumatized twenty-year-old unwed mother. It wasn't right what Shirley had done, but Brinna still appreciated the good that Shirley and her mother had done despite all the bad.

"Your family has a lot to work through right now, Shirley," Brinna said, offering a kind smile. "I'll be praying for you. And if you need anything... I'm here."

"We all are," Ben added.

Gabe gave Brinna a grateful smile. She knew he didn't want to embarrass the Boystons any more than was necessary, so she took a deep breath and rounded up the troops. She'd get them back down to the party so Zoey and Ben could finish out the evening with their friends. No one would even notice that Shirley and Renner were being led away by a cop.

It was too bad, though. Brinna had been having a really good time with that cop. The party wouldn't be the same without Gabe. Nothing would. The investigation was over now, and he would no longer need her assistance. Was this it for them?

She glanced at him one last time as she followed Zoey and Ben out the door. Her cheeks burned as she realized he'd been watching her, too. She was sure Gabe had been enjoying their time together as much as she had.

Maybe there would be other parties they could laugh together at. She hoped so.

SEVENTEEN

The wedding was lovely. Gabe had been nervous about being such an important part of Ben and Zoey's day after the tension he'd felt with Ben during the investigation, but the hard feelings were gone. After the truth came out at the party, Ben was much more understanding about Gabe's actions toward the Boystons, as well as his involvement with Brinna. Today, in fact, Ben seemed perfectly happy to see Gabe enjoying the reception with Brinna at his side.

Brinna and Zoey were back to being best friends again, and Gabe was happy for them. Truth had a wonderful way of restoring trust. Shirley and Renner had been at the wedding, but they'd opted not to attend the reception. While neither of them had been charged with any crimes at this point, the whole town was abuzz with the news about Barty's death and the fact that his body had been hidden all these years. Shirley had already announced she was stepping down as CEO. Drexel would move into an executive position, as would Ben.

It was good to know the company would still be in good hands. Porter Swenson had chosen to stay in town for a while to get to know his half brother and do research for a book he actually intended to write. After learning the facts of his father's disappearance, he'd decided he might want to be a mystery writer now.

Brinna's grandfather was beaming now that he'd been officially exonerated in the embezzlement scandal. He was especially proud that it had been his own grandchildren who'd found the proof of his innocence. She had made sure to tell him that it was his silly password code that had ended up saving the day on that account.

As for Brinna, she'd been basking in the joy of knowing that she'd done what she'd set out to do. Yes, she'd been a huge part of solving the fifty-year-old cold case, but more importantly, she'd given her grandfather back his good name. Gabe knew Brinna well, and he understood that this was priceless to her. She was perfectly happy to go back to her archives and forget all about investigations and mysteries now. Not that he wouldn't value her help on any future cases.

Gabe leaned back in the folding chair. The day's festivities were winding down. Bright music still played in the background, and giggling children still ran in circles through the reception hall, unconcerned about keeping their fancy clothes neat. Brinna had gone off to help Zoey change out of her expensive and elaborate wedding gown into whatever expensive and elaborate outfit she wanted to wear for her grand departure. Caterers were clearing the dinner plates and consolidating foods on the buffet tables. Alone for the time being, Gabe soaked in the joy he felt all around him.

"You seem to actually be having a good time," his father said, lowering himself into an empty seat.

"I am. How about you?"

"Great time. It feels like ages since I've been a wedding guest and not just the preacher."

"It's nice that Kay was able to drive you today since I had to get to the church so early. If she needs to head out, though, I can drive you home when you're ready."

"Um, about that… I don't think you quite understand things with me and Kay."

"She's been helping you out with things, and I really appreciate that."

"So do I. But she's not just some nice lady taking pity on me, Gabe. I'm not an invalid anymore. Kay and I have been friends for a long time now, and we spent a lot of time together even before I had that stroke."

"I know, Dad. And that's great. I like Kay a lot."

"Do you? I hope so, because we've been talking about the future. *Our* future. Together."

"What? You and Kay?"

"Don't look so amazed. I've still got it."

Gabe couldn't help but laugh. "Of course you do. And you should totally have someone to share it with. Congratulations. Is there anything set yet?"

"I asked her to marry me, and she said yes... provided you approve."

"I do, Dad. I absolutely do."

His father nearly glowed with happiness as he pulled himself up from the chair. "Good. Then I guess I'll go tell her that it's time to get ready for another wedding. I don't suppose you'd like to make it a double? I've seen the way you and Brinna have been looking at each other..."

"Didn't you warn me not to spend too much time with her?"

"Yes, and you clearly ignored me. But since she's not told you to hit the road even now that she's done helping you with that murder stuff, I guess I didn't need to warn you after all. If that girl hasn't given up on you after all this time, maybe she never will. And that's something worth hanging on to."

"We'll see. We'll see if there's hope I can fix all the things I messed up."

"Just so you know, Gabe, you don't have to fix it all on your own."

"I know, Dad. And thanks. Now go spend time with your fiancée."

His dad was still chuckling to himself over the word *fiancée* as he headed off to find Kay. Gabe shook his head. So he was going to have a stepmother after all this time. He'd never really thought about his father remarrying. He should have, though. He should've thought of a lot of other people instead of being so self-centered. It was wonderful to see Dad so happy now. Kay was a good woman, and they made a good team.

"What are you grinning about?" Brinna said, sliding into the chair his father had just vacated.

"You'll never believe it. My father and Kay Hefler are getting married."

Instead of swooning with surprise, Brinna just rolled her eyes. "Finally. They've been perfect for each other for years."

"You saw this coming?"

"Of course. Didn't you?"

"No, I have to admit I did not."

Brinna laughed at him. "Clueless. Come on. Ben and Zoey are getting ready to leave. We need to say goodbye and see how the groomsmen have decorated Ben's car. I heard rumors about duct tape, Christmas lights, and rubber chickens."

"That'll be interesting. Okay, lead the way."

She took his hand and headed for the door. He gladly followed, wondering if she had any idea how comfortable her hand felt in his. How on earth had he ever walked away from her? If his father was right, and leaving was something he'd needed to do at the time, he prayed that the lessons he'd needed to learn had been worth it.

They gathered with the rest of the guests out in front of the building. Everyone had been given a tiny bottle of bubble solution, so when the happy couple emerged, they found themselves in a blizzard of iridescent bubbles. There were cheers, hugs, and happy tears. Eventually, Ben and Zoey got into his humorously decorated car and drove away. The bubbles faded, and the crowd began to disperse.

"I'd say that was a success," Gabe noted, happy to linger outside in the glow of the sunset that filtered red and gold through the trees.

"Yeah. It was a perfect day. I know they're going to be very happy together."

They stood together, leaning against the railing that overlooked the lush green gardens of the beautiful reception hall. With all the excitement of the day over, most people were leaving. Before long, Brinna would probably want to go home, too, and life would go back to normal. Gabe would have no excuse to spend time with her, aside from just running into her at community events or shopping for groceries. If he wanted to see Brinna, he was going to have to ask her out.

He'd been to war, and he'd done some frightening things. Asking Brinna if she would go out with him on a real, intentional date was by far the most terrifying. What if she said no?

He would just have to accept it if she did. If he'd been bold enough to break her heart ten years ago, he could certainly be bold enough to let her break his tonight. He cleared his throat, yet his voice still cracked like a nervous teenager.

"Um, Brinna?"

"Yeah?"

"Do you… I mean, now that we're done with the investigation and all the wedding events, do you think we could go out for dinner or something?"

"You're still hungry? We just had a pretty big meal, Gabe."

"No, I didn't mean tonight, I meant… Look, I have really enjoyed working with you, spending time with you. I'd like to keep doing that. I know you have plenty of reason to be done with me, but I would love it if you'd give me a second chance."

She blinked up at him. "A second chance? What does that mean? You want a second chance to go out? To get to be each other's best friend? To fall in love? To plan a wedding?"

"Yes, I want a second chance for everything.

For going out, for planning a wedding, for making a home, for getting old together… All of it."

He held his breath, praying that she wouldn't yell *no*! and run off in the other direction. She didn't. Instead, to his surprise, she started laughing.

"Okay…that wasn't supposed to be a joke," he said slowly.

"I'm sorry," she said, trying to contain herself. "I'm not laughing at you, Gabe. I'm laughing at myself. I'm such a coward. All day, I've been thinking up clever excuses to keep you from walking out of my life. Maybe I'll just happen to stop by the police station, or maybe I'll get you to come by the library for some silly reason. Maybe I'll run a few stop signs and hope you're the one who pulls me over."

"Oh, I don't recommend that."

"No, I disregarded that one right away. But seriously, Gabe, it never dawned on me to be brave enough to come right out and tell you the truth. I don't want to need silly excuses to see you. I want to see you because you like being with me. I want that second chance—for everything."

"Well, you don't ever have to worry about needing excuses to see me. I *do* like being with you, Brinna. I love you, in fact. If that's not what you want, I'm afraid you'll need silly excuses to get rid of me."

She laughed again but stepped closer to him. "How about if we give up on the excuses and just focus on truth. I still love you, and I believe we can make things work. I just thought it was going to take a little while to get you to realize that."

"Oh, I realized that right away," he said and put his arms around her. "If I ever did stop loving you, I fell right back into it the minute I saw you again. I hope I'm a better man now, though. I've done a lot of growing up."

"We both have. I don't know if this is the path God had planned for us from the start, or if everything just brought us back to it, but I know this is exactly where we're supposed to be now."

"Me, too," Gabe said, meeting her gaze. "So… is it too soon to ask you to marry me?"

"Will you actually show up on the day of the wedding?"

"I will chain myself to the front pew if it'll make you more comfortable."

She laughed. "No need for that. I never thought I'd say this, but I trust you, Gabe Elliot. I love you, and I trust you. And yes, I *will* marry you."

He knew she had worked through quite a lot to feel that way after what he'd done. He realized that he'd worked through a lot, too. He would never have told her how he really felt or asked her to marry him if he didn't truly trust that he could follow through. He'd finally forgiven him-

self. He could have that second chance for a lifetime with Brinna.

"I'll be there for you, Brinna. Today, tomorrow, ten years from now, in our old age, and on
our wedding day. I promise."

"Not necessarily in that order, I hope." She
laughed as she stood on her tiptoes to kiss him.

It was more than he could have hoped for. Despite everything, Brinna was in his arms again
and wanted to be by his side for life. He had no
doubt they would stand together at that altar and
make their vows, ten years late, but right on time.

* * * * *

Dear Reader,

I hope you love Brinna and Gabe just as much as I do. These two have gone through a lot: abandonment, public accusations, the illness of loved ones, their struggles to hold on to faith. It broke my heart to write about Gabe's pain and regret over his past choices, but I was inspired by Brinna's growth and the way God brought her through heartbreak to discover a side of her she didn't even know existed. It was rewarding to help them along on their journey back to each other.

Sometimes bad things happen, and life doesn't go the way we plan. Sometimes we're innocent victims, and sometimes it's our own foolishness that causes the chaos. Always, though, God is right there with us. I hope you feel Him with you today, loving you, forgiving you, and guiding you along your path.

With His love,
Susan Gee Heino

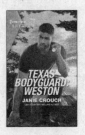